THE GODS HATE KANSAS

THE GODS HATE KANSAS

JOSEPH J. MILLARD

WILDSIDE PRESS

CHAPTER 1

Rock Fall

The rocks had been hurtling toward Earth for more than a week, silent and invisible in the black, airless void of space. There were eleven of the dark chunks, each roughly the size of a basketball. In appearance they were no different from other random meteoric fragments that occasionally whipped past them at vastly greater speeds.

The eleven, however, could not be mistaken for cosmic debris. There was too clearly an intelligent purpose in the pattern of their flight, maintaining an unvarying arrowhead formation as the tens of thousands of trackless miles fled by. There was added evidence in their fixed speed of precisely nineteen miles per second.

The rocks were nearing the Earth now, still invisible but reacting to the first faint pull of gravity. Directly beneath lay the parched and dusty reaches of the Kansas Plains.

* * * *

August Solle was pitching bedding straw into the last of a row of cow stalls when he heard his wife's voice calling from the house: "Supper's ready. Come and get it." He leaned the pitchfork against the wall, snapped off the barn light and stepped outside, slapping loose straw from his sun-faded overalls.

The night was clear and moonless. The air still held a remnant of the day's heat and the faint smell of dust. August Solle tipped his head back and studied the blazing canopy of stars overhead, a helpless anger settling over his gaunt, tired face with its bleached eyebrows and stubble of graying whiskers.

Young Gus, his gangling twenty-year-old son, came out of the machine shed, dusting his hands, and stood waiting for Arnie Cole, the hired man, to join him. Together they walked toward the elder Solle. In the kitchen door Martha Solle waited, her spare figure outlined against the light.

"What you looking for, Pa?" Gus asked.

"A miracle, I guess. I keep lookin' to find just one measly little patch of cloud so's we can hope for a drop of rain. I've never see a spring as dry as this one."

5

"If we don't get rain by the end of the week," Arnie Cole said glumly, "there won't be no use in planting wheat this year. I swear, the more I see of Kansas, the more I wish I'd never left Ioway."

Solle dragged a long sigh from the depths of his work-worn body. "It's got so I've even took to getting up in the night to look for clouds. But all I ever see are them goldanged stars. I never thought I'd get to hate the sight of stars."

He glared resentfully at the blazing splendor overhead and the others, in unconscious imitation, threw their heads back to follow his gaze. In the kitchen door, Martha Solle looked skyward to see what the men were gazing at.

Thus it happened that four pairs of eyes were watching at the precise moment when, some eighty-seven miles above the Earth, the rocks first glowed to incandescence under the lash of tenuous atmosphere.

"Look!" Martha cried. "Shooting stars—a flock of 'em."

"Meteors, Ma," Gus corrected, his voice cracking with excitement. "A meteor swarm. We studied about 'em in school."

Then there was no longer time for speech. The leisurely glide of outer space had become, in relation to Earth, a whipping flight. In two seconds the flaming V was close enough for the naked eye to separate its eleven component masses. In three seconds, the individual rocks appeared larger than baseballs and their color had changed from dull red to blinding white.

With a crashing thunder that shook the Earth and tortured eardrums, the rocks burst through the sonic barrier as mounting friction dragged down their speed. From somewhere in the house came the tinkle and clatter of falling glass.

Then there were two lesser but deafening explosions as two of the rocks succumbed to the titanic forces of kinetic energy and burst apart in midair. The remaining nine flashed downward, their arrowhead formation unchanged despite two gaps.

The Solles and Arnie Cole stood frozen, locked in a paralysis of mingled awe and fright. Now it seemed to their bulging eyes that the nine flaming rocks were arrowing straight at the house. A strangled, incoherent yell burst from August Solle's lips.

Then miraculously the arrowing rocks were flashing just above the roof, down over the rooted four and beyond. The awesome roar of their passage deafened them and a breath of superheated air seared the upturned faces.

The next instant the rocks struck and buried themselves in the edge of the unplanted wheat field barely ten rods beyond. Dust and fire and fearful sound burst up and the ground underfoot shook from the impact. The spreading shock wave hit and knocked the four to the ground. For a moment they were buffeted by a secondary wave of scorching air, a furnace blast that swept them and was gone, racing out into the night.

Then there was only stillness, broken by the patter of falling fragments from the exploded rocks. Blinded, deafened, choking and terrified, the four witnesses clung to the parched ground.

August Solle was the first to regain speech. "Martha, are you all right? Gus? Amie?"

"I—I think so," Martha croaked.

The others mumbled agreement as they broke the spell and scrambled erect on shaky legs. Young Gus found his voice and wits. "Jumping Judas! Come on! They landed right over there at the edge of the plowed part, Pa. Hurry!"

"Wait," Martha cried shakily. "The others might blow up, too. You'd best not go near, at least for a while."

"They won't," Gus yelled wildly. "Don't you know what we got, Ma? They're worth money and they're all ours. Remember when Pete Halvorson found just a little chunk of an old meteorite a couple years ago and a man from Washington paid him fifty bucks for it? We must have hundreds of dollars worth—maybe even thousands—right here in our own field."

He whirled and ran toward the great cloud of dust that was settling slowly back over the line of raw scars where the alien rocks had slammed into the Earth. The others ran with him, the prospect of buried treasure overriding their fears.

In the nine shallow pits along the edge of the field the *things* lay quietly, waiting…

CHAPTER 2

Meteor Menace

At three o'clock in the morning the telephone set up its unholy jangling in the bachelor apartment of Curtis Temple, Professor of Astrophysics and Meteoritics at Culwain University. He fumbled out into the darkness and found the light switch, muttering unacademic comments. Yawning, he levered his rangy six-feet-one to a vertical position and lifted the phone.

The voice of the university night operator sounded sleepy and aggrieved. "Oh, Dr. Temple, I didn't want to disturb you at such an awful hour, but the operator says it's some kind of emergency. It's a long distance call from Washington, a Mr. Van Arden at National Aeronautics and Space Administration."

Temple lowered the phone, examined it with sleepy suspicion and put it back to his ear. "He's got the wrong number."

A brusque, commanding voice cut through the line noises. "Temple? Van Arden at NASA. What's your personal opinion of last night's show?"

"Show?" Temple echoed, his face slack. "Are you drunk?"

"Damn it!" Van Arden shouted. "Don't you astronomers out there ever *look* at the sky? You had the most spectacular meteor show of the century last night. Eleven fireballs popped into sight over New Mexico, and sailed northeast. Two exploded in the air but the other nine struck on the farm of a man named Solle, twenty miles west of Bomer, Kansas."

Temple was suddenly wide-awake, his blue eyes very bright. He snatched pad and pen from the night stand. "We're over three hundred miles away so we couldn't see it, and early reports probably went to Flagstaff Observatory first. How did you get it in Washington so fast?"

"Hah!" Van Arden said. "Our Missile-Warning radar net got the blips from outer space and threw the whole Defense Command into a flap. SAC scrambled all bombers, the White House went on alert and opened the Moscow phone line and STRIKE had its finger on the dirty-bird button. We've still got the nuclear shakes."

"I can understand that," Temple said, scribbling furiously, "What I don't get is where I fit into your picture?"

"Smithsonian says you're a top authority on Meteoritics, with some kind of flying squad of picked scientists set up to rush to a meteorite

8

fall and find out what they're made of and where they came from."

"We have a Meteoritics Field Team with a portable laboratory for on-the spot analysis. We'll certainly want to get in on this fall if the university will stand the expense—"

"Damn the expense!" Van Arden snapped. "NASA will foot all the bills. You just get 'em there as fast as you can. The local sheriff's guarding the site now and I'm leaving by jet in half an hour. How fast can you make it?"

"Sometime this afternoon," Temple said, calculating the problems. "But what's your angle on all this? I thought NASA's big interest was shooting things into space. When did you get hotted up over something *from* space?"

"When that something travels in perfect V-formation, like a fleet of vehicles…or guided missiles," Van Arden said grimly and hung up.

Temple stared at the black rectangle of his window, his mind working furiously. He was not greatly impressed by the implications of Van Arden's last remark. So little was actually known about meteorites even yet that the arrival of a swarm waving flags and playing an extra-galactic anthem would not be too staggering a surprise.

The existence of nine whole, fresh meteorites waiting to be studied was infinitely more exciting. Of an estimated 24 million that strike Earth's atmosphere every day, no more than four or five fragments of any size were recovered in an average year. Most of these were not found until vital clues to their nature and origin had been lost or weathered away. The infant science of Meteoritics was built almost entirely from ancient falls and a study of the meteoric dust in the atmosphere. Now suddenly a thousand burning questions might be answered on a Kansas farm.

From the night he had first gaped in childish awe at a fireball streaking across the sky, Curtis Temple had been obsessed by a fierce need to plumb the mysteries of these aliens from space. By the time he was in high school he had absorbed everything printed on the subject. In college he swallowed Astronomy and Astrophysics in great gulps, achieving his Ph.D. at the mature age of 26. Now, at 30, he was an acknowledged authority and one of the pioneers in establishing Meteoritics as a separate science.

Five months before, his passion had almost cost him his life when the plane in which he was collecting meteoric dust crashed on a cloud-swathed mountain. When pulled from the wreckage, doctors had given him a slender one-in-ten chance of survival. Now, thanks to his toughness and their skill in rebuilding a shattered skull with a silver plate, he was almost whole again.

He blinked and pulled himself down from the cloudland of anticipation to the demands of the immediate moment. Grinning faintly, he dialed Lee Mason's number.

In spite of himself, his mind pictured her reluctant awakening. He hoped her honey-blond hair would be in a becoming tangle, not trapped in hideous curlers. Her face, he knew, would be warm and lovely even without make-up and she would probably be wearing something thin and frilly that did nothing to hide the softly rounded curves.

Temple hastily pulled his imagination off that delicate vision. When the last classes ended in mid-June, he and Lee would stand in the university chapel and say the words that would make such intimate details no longer wistful conjecture.

Meanwhile, Lee Mason was his department assistant and a respected scientist in her own right. She knew almost as much about his specialty as he did and was, in addition, a recognized authority on astronautics problems. One of the professors had described Lee Mason with classic clarity. "Nature outdid herself when she packed brains like that in such an attractive package. You're a lucky, lucky guy, Curt."

The ringing stopped and Lee's sleep-drugged voice mumbled something. Temple chuckled. "Rise and shine, baby doll. The Meteoritics Team is on the march."

"Curt!" Her voice was abruptly alert. "There's been a meteorite fall within our range?"

"A perfect gee-whiz of a composite fall, hon." He reported Van Arden's call. "Meet me at the lab as fast as you can. We've got to arouse the team and wake McCabe to get clearance."

Lee giggled. "Let me call McCabe. I've always wondered what kind of language a pompous university president would use when he's rousted out of bed at four A.M."

"Granted," Temple said. He grinned. "Tell me one thing, Lee. What are you wearing right this moment?"

He heard a gasp, then a giggle. "The answer to that could set meteorics back ten years. Keep your mind on your work."

* * * *

It was only a few minutes past eight in the morning when the last of the four Culwain University trucks rumbled southward, carrying the prefab huts, portable generator, heavy tools and supplies, and the delicate instruments and equipment for the Meteoritics Field Laboratory. A jeep and a station wagon waited to take the team members with their personal belongings and a few excessively fragile pieces.

The five team members were as excited as schoolboys on a camp-out at the prospect. Each was an authority in his own field—chemistry, physics, petrography, geology, biology—each prepared and equipped to follow any relationship to his own specialty through to an informative conclusion. Temple and Lee, as a team, had the task of collating the diverse bits of information into a coherent picture of the mysterious strangers from space.

Temple was rechecking the last lists when his telephone rang. Lee answered, listened in silence for several minutes, then handed the instrument across the worktable. Temple was too preoccupied to notice the expression on her face.

The voice of University President McCabe sounded strained. "Curtis, after approving the expedition you called about this morning, I took the precaution of contacting the head surgeon at University Hospital. He—if I may be permitted a slang expression—blew his cork at your intention to participate in such a rigorous activity at this time. He says such a move could cost you your health, if not your life. In short, he expressly forbade your leaving his watch and care."

"Wha-a-t?" Temple yelled. "I'm perfectly well and I feel great. All that skull carpenter wants is more pictures of my head for his private collection. Tell him to keep his cotton-picking fingers to hell out of my business. When he let me out of the hospital, he ended his right to run my life."

"Precisely," McCabe said stiffly. "That is why he left the decision to me. By virtue of your contract, I still retain a certain right and I'm afraid, on his advice, I must exercise it against my will. Your leave of absence is hereby canceled. You will be expected to remain on campus and conduct your lectures as usual until further notice." He added, very softly, "I wish I could tell you how sorry I am, Curtis."

The last kit and case were packed, the team ready to leave a few minutes before nine. In the laboratory doorway Lee stood for a moment, looking at Temple's harsh face and dull eyes as he shook the last hand, mouthed the last good wishes.

Suddenly she whirled and threw herself against him, hugging his taut body fiercely, feeling its slow, unwilling yielding to her warmth.

"Curt, oh, Curt," she whispered, "please don't take it so hard. It isn't the end of the world. It's still your research, all of it. I'll air-mail a full, detailed report of everything that's done there, every single day, by every one of the team. We'll take photographs and draw charts and graphs so you won't miss a single clue. And every single evening, between six and seven, I'll telephone you. I promise, Curt. You'll be much too busy, and I'll be close enough, so you won't have time to get lonely or blue."

She whispered, "Until tonight, darling," kissed him hard and ran to

11

the waiting car.

It was not her fault, nor his, that the promise on which they parted was so quickly and viciously broken.

CHAPTER 3

Sinister Rocks

For five days, Temple found little time to brood over his bitter disappointment. Each mail brought a great bundle of detailed information from Lee, as well as photos, sketches and eye-witness reports from Flagstaff Observatory and its network of meteor watch teams. Shortly after six each evening there was a long, heart-warming telephone visit, not only with Lee but with any of the others who had problems or theories to discuss.

On the fifth night there was no phone call; on the next day, no mail or contact of any kind. Temple was only kept from doing something rash by the calm wisdom of Dr. Tom Mullane, the wizened, gnome-like little Dean of Astronomy who shared office and laboratory space in the same Observatory wing.

"Be reasonable, Curt. I've seen you so preoccupied with an interesting problem that you forgot to eat or sleep. If I know that bunch of fanatics, they're so engrossed in cracking their space eggs and peering inside that they've forgotten that such things as telephones and reports exist. If there'd been an accident or any kind of trouble, you'd have been the first to hear of it."

"Okay, okay, Granny," Temple said. He grinned sheepishly. "I'll be calm and collected and reasonable—for one more day. Then if I don't hear anything—*Bango!*"

Mullane laughed. "Sure you don't mean *gr-r-rowr-r-r*, Tiger? I remember my courting days. But I'll buy it as is, and tomorrow I'll stay clear of the blast area. Now let's finish our backtracking on the trajectory of that swarm and see if we can establish what part of space they came from." An hour later they threw down pencils almost simultaneously and stared at one another across the big worktable in Temple's office. Temple said at last, "Are you absolutely sure, Mully?"

"Positive," Mullane said flatly. "As far as I'm concerned the impossible is incontrovertible fact. Your meteorites could have come from only one place in the universe—the surface of the moon. You have more than enough verified observations to establish the point and altitude of entry into atmosphere, their velocity and angle of descent. Unless some force caused that swarm to change course and speed somewhere in space, they could not possibly have originated at any other point."

"I agree," Temple said, and reached for the telephone. "All bets are off, Mully. I'm calling Lee right now to warn her of what Van Arden only suspected…if it isn't too late."

His hand was closing on the instrument when it rang. He snatched it up. The voice of University President McCabe had a ragged note of near hysteria in it. "Temple, get over here as fast as you can. Your field team in Kansas—"

"What about the field team?" Temple shouted.

"You'd better be prepared to tell *me*," McCabe cried. "I think they've gone mad, stark, raving mad. They have brought financial ruin to themselves and to Culwain University—*utter financial ruin.*"

* * * *

To Lee Mason the site of the meteorite fall resembled a circus she remembered from childhood, one that had arrived in the night and was half set up when she saw it at dawn.

The Culwain trucks had arrived earlier. A row of portable huts was going up, five as dormitories for team and work crew, one as kitchen and storeroom, the largest as joint laboratory and work space. The generator was running to supply power to cables of various sizes which snaked across the dusty ground.

She had not expected such a crowd. The line of impact pits was roped off and surrounded by a thin line of faintly self-conscious men wearing deputy's badges. Around that were some uniformed State Police and, cautiously back from them, a number of strangers she eventually learned were FBI and CIA men. Outside this secondary ring were reporters, curiosity seekers, a TV news team and various strangers never identified.

A huge, blond man pushed up. "Meteoritics Team? What the hell kept you? Where the hell is this Temple character?" He suddenly discovered Lee and amended hastily, "I mean, where might I find Dr. Temple, the Meteoritics expert?"

Lee decided correctly that this was Van Arden. "I'm sorry but he was unable to accompany the team and sent me to take his place." She explained about Temple's recent injuries and introduced the members of the team. Van Arden shook hands, looking a little like a man who felt he was not getting his money's worth.

"You've only got about four hours of daylight left and that may not be enough time to dig out all the meteorites, or whatever they are. Hadn't you better set your work crew to rigging floodlights now so you won't be interrupted later on?"

Lee looked at him sharply. "I'm afraid you don't understand our

14

work, Mr. Van Arden. It will be days before we're set to bring out the meteorites themselves, or even expose them to view. Our first work will be to extract all possible information from the impact craters and the surrounding soil. Until that is done we can't risk destroying vital clues by digging."

Van Arden glared around the circle of faces, then turned and stamped off, muttering to himself. Jacobs, the chubby analytical chemist, broke the silence with a snort.

"Bureaucrats! What does he expect us to find down there anyhow, little green men?"

"Or Khrushchev's fingerprints," Lee said.

"Shucks," Jacobs said. "I forgot to bring my Junior G-Man Kit."

The Solles and Amie Cole, reassured that they would be paid for all meteoritic material, proved most co-operative. The men joined the Culwain work crew and Martha Solle took over the cooking. By the time Lee telephoned Temple the camp was set up and lighted and much of the equipment unpacked. Van Arden held a long talk and emerged looking a little sheepish.

When work began at sunup, he hovered close, keeping out of the way and speaking little but looking both intrigued and baffled. He trudged along, scowling, watching Lee and the prim little refugee physicist, Dr. Eno Rocossen, wheel a device like a futuristic mine detector along the north edge of the impact pits. Both wore earphones and kept an intent watch on a row of dials. At the end of the row of pits they snapped switches and removed the headphones.

"Stonies," Rocossen said. "It is not of surprise, no?"

Lee nodded. "The gods still hate Kansas, it seems."

"What the devil does that mean?" Van Arden blurted.

"Curt—Dr. Temple—coined a phrase long ago from one of the unsolved mysteries of Meteoritics," Lee explained, smiling. "He says the gods must hate Kansas, since they throw so many stones at it. Broadly, meteorites fall into three types, according to their composition. Siderites are mainly iron, aerolites are stone, and siderolites are composed of both iron and stone. These appear to be all aerolites, or stones."

"I get it. That gadget's a kind of glorified mine detector that would show the presence of metal. But what's this 'gods hate Kansas' business?"

"For a reason no scientist can explain, more stony meteorites strike little Kansas than any other place on Earth. One-third of all known North American aerolite falls, and one-sixth of those reported in the world, have been in Kansas. Despite a sparse population, more falls have been witnessed in Kansas than anywhere else on Earth. Kansas receives more stones than any other state, more than any two states

15

west of the Mississippi. Now we have nine new ones to push the imbalance even further."

Van Arden blinked dazedly and emitted a long whistle. "With puzzles like that to solve, I don't wonder you couldn't get too excited over a little thing like a V-formation flight."

The work went on in orderly confusion. The funnel-shaped craters were meticulously sketched, photographed and their angles measured. Steel probes marked the location, extent and depth of the buried meteorites, which because of the angle of impact lay some distance beyond the pit openings.

Soil samples were taken at varying depths. Chemical analysis could determine the degree of heat generated at impact and the presence of any fragments of crust spalled off. Microbiology searched for traces of alien microorganisms. An intricate machine delivered measured blows on the plowed ground to determine its resistance and estimate thereby the probable velocity of the rocks at the moment of impact. The work crew scoured the Earth for fragments of the exploded aerolites. Each team member carried a portable tape recorder and there were frequent halts to sketch or photograph possibly significant findings.

By the third day Van Arden's respect had grown and so had his impatience. He cornered Lee Mason during a brief coffee break.

"Have a heart, lady. I don't want to make a pest of myself, but tell me if you've run across *anything* that's different from ordinary meteorites."

Lee studied him thoughtfully, then nodded. "We may have. It may not mean a thing because we still know so little about the field that no one can say what an ordinary meteorite is. But the Geiger counter and scintillometer show these aerolites to be more radioactive than any previously known." She checked his outburst with a lifted hand. "It's nowhere near the danger level. Other stonies have been only about a fourth as radioactive as common terrestrial granite, which isn't much. In this case, the difference is very small, but there *is* a difference. We may learn more when they're examined in the lab."

Van Arden mopped his forehead. "For Pete's sake, hurry it up, will you? Only a handful of top brass in Washington knows what I'm looking for here, but that handful is getting jumpier by the hour."

They hurried, but it was not until the afternoon of the fifth day that preliminary study was finished and the actual exhumation of the aerolites was begun.

It was dark by the time the digging was finished and the last stone exposed. The floods were turned on and by their light Gus Solle used the farm tractor to snake the nine great globular rocks from their pits to a wooden platform beside the laboratory building.

16

There was a concerted rush by the whole group to examine the stones more closely. Lee, on her knees beside the largest, frowned in bewilderment. Van Arden pushed through and knelt beside her. "So these things really are different from anything your experience led you to expect. Right?"

"Yes," Lee said. She ran her fingertips over the dark surface. "This isn't any normal fusion surface. It's—it's as if a round rock had been dipped in black pitch. Nothing like this has ever been reported before. And they're all alike in appearance."

"Like a protective coating," Van Arden asked softly, "that had been artificially applied, maybe?"

Lee looked at him dazedly. "Yes. That's exactly how they look."

Bensil, the petrographer, crowded in between them with a geologist's hammer. "There's only one way to determine whether or not this is a coating. Give me room to swing and I'll chip off a fragment. We'll want to save the grinding and etching for daylight, anyhow."

"Hold it," Van Arden said sharply. "Somebody switch off the lights for a second."

There was a click, then a gasp. In the darkness, the nine aerolites glowed with a soft, greenish radiance. A babble of excited comment burst from the group. The lights blazed on again.

"Thanks," Van Arden said. "I thought I caught a glimpse of fluorescence when you leaned over and shaded it. I'm an administrator, not a scientist, but there's something about these damn lumps that doesn't look kosher to me—not kosher at all."

Suddenly Lee Mason swayed and started to fall forward. Bensil dropped his hammer and caught her. "Lee, what's the matter? Are you ill?"

She straightened with an effort and gave him a wan smile. "I'm all right, Mark. For a moment I had the most frightening feeling that—that something would happen if we were to crack that shell. I'm all right now, though. It was just nerves, and too much excitement."

"You know what's the matter with you?" Bensil chuckled as he retrieved the hammer. "Guilty conscience, honey. You were so excited over these rocks that you forgot to phone Curt at the usual time tonight. Wait until I crack this shell and we may have a real story to bend his ear with."

He swung the hammer. There was a sharp crack, and a chip of black flew off, revealing the familiar gray-brown of meteoric rock beneath.

For a moment Van Arden thought he saw a soundless flash of light from the impact. No one else seemed to have noticed it.

With deft swings, Bensil broke chips from the remaining aerolites. Lee followed, carefully putting each into a tight envelope bearing the

17

same identifying number that had been painted onto the rock before it left its pit. They all followed her, crowding into the laboratory where the first rough preliminary chemical, microscopic and spectrographic analysis would be run.

Recovered from her momentary weakness, Lee stood holding the envelopes, smiling as she looked around the circle of tense, excited faces. "I won't phone Curt just yet. This may be an epic night in the history of Meteoritics. We'll start by—"

She staggered, caught hold of the corner of a laboratory bench and clung there, her face screwed into an expression of agony. The nine envelopes scattered on the floor at her feet. Van Arden swore thickly and started to push toward her. The others seemed to be rooted, too stunned to move.

Lee straightened suddenly and smiled. "It's quite all right now. There is a brief moment of dizziness when the connection is first made, but it passes almost immediately. Control of musculature and vocal chords seems awkward but adequate. You may all choose your subjects and connect."

"What the hell?" Van Arden roared. "What's going on—?"

He stopped short, writhing, clawing at the back of his neck. Like a dash of ice water, something indescribably cold touched and clung there. He slapped at it but his hand found nothing.

His muscles refused to answer the command of his will. He staggered, feeling as if icicles were being driven deep into the back of his skull, into the very matter and substance of his brain. For a moment he was caught in a wave of unutterable agony. Through the waves of pain he heard the voice of Lee Mason, curiously without warmth or life, saying:

"I had been doubtful of my choice of vehicle, but it turns out to be excellent. The brain is all anyone could ask of these primitives. In addition, I learn from suppressed images that even the curious conformation of this one's body has its unique influence over the actions of other bipeds who are not quite similarly formed. I believe I have made a most excellent choice."

From some infinite depth of horror, Van Arden heard his own deep voice saying, "Connection complete and quite satisfactory. We can now proceed with the next step of the plan."

CHAPTER 4

Meteor Madness

Curtis Temple glared at Culwain University's President, Cyrus McCabe. His own fears and worries had driven him beyond the point of discretion. "Stop that idiot babbling and make sense. What do you mean, our Meteoritics Team has gone off its rocker? What's happened to them? What have they done?"

Cyrus McCabe had been noted as the perfect picture of the politician-administrator who could both manage and finance a growing educational institution. Now, Temple thought in a flash of cynical realism, he looked like a Bowery bum. His mane of silvery hair was rumpled, his pink jowls slack and quivering, his eyes red-veined. His hand shook as he pushed a pile of papers across his desk.

"Look at these," he croaked. "Just *look* at them."

Temple snatched the sheaf, thumbed through it, and began to feel the way McCabe looked. Every one was an invoice, charged to Culwain University and signed by one or another of his team. Most were from cities in Kansas, for lumber, cement, steel, reinforcing bars, electrical equipment.

"Now, take it easy," Temple said, trying to force himself to swallow the same advice. "Obviously, this is material needed for some emergency research. After all, NASA did agree to foot the bills, and Van Arden is there with them."

"Research?" McCabe cried wildly. "Miles of interlocking steel-mesh fence with insulated posts? Enough heavy-duty electric cable to wire this whole campus? And look at this—"

Temple could only gape wordlessly at invoices for sawed-off shotguns, submachine guns, automatic pistols, tear gas grenades, every one signed with the unmistakable heart-wrenching signature of Lee Mason. He managed to mumble weakly, "Now, we must not jump to conclusions, sir. Obviously their investigation has led them to something unusual and valuable."

"Oh, obviously," McCabe cried. "A little while ago, Mrs. Eno Rocossen telephoned me. She was in tears. She had tried to cash a small check on their joint account and discovered Eno had closed out both their savings and checking accounts to the last penny. Ten minutes later Mrs. Jacobs called with the same complaint."

"Why would they do that?" Temple mumbled blankly.

"You explain it," McCabe shouted. "I checked and every man on your team has done the same. So has your precious Lee Mason. But that isn't the worst of it."

"Oh, no," Temple said dazedly. "I'm afraid to ask what is."

"Before they left I gave Dr. Rocossen a blank check on our operating account to cover emergencies that might arise. I had complete faith in his honesty and integrity. But what did he do? He drew out every cent of our operating funds—to the last penny. We can't pay salaries, buy supplies, even meet our current bills. We're—we're *bankrupt*." He threw up his hands. "I tried to phone them and no one will talk to me."

"They'll talk to me," Temple shouted, coming out of his trance. "By phone or in person, they'll talk."

He dialed the operator and placed a call to the number of the Solle farm, which Lee had sent him the first day. After an eternity of jingles, hums, clicks, the sharp, nasal voice of a woman answered.

"I'd like to talk to Miss Lee Mason on the Meteoritics Team, or any of the men if she isn't immediately available."

"Ain't here," the woman said.

Temple sensed that she was about to hang up and shouted. "Wait a minute. What do you mean, they're not there? They're camped right there in your yard. If they're not there now, where are they? When will they be back?"

"Didn't say," the nasal voice snapped. There was a *click* and the line went dead.

Temple yelled into emptiness until a disembodied voice came on. "Your party has hung up. Were you disconnected?"

"Yes," Temple shouted. "No—I mean, I wasn't finished. Call that number back."

A monotonous ringing went on and on until finally the metallic voice cut in. "Your number does not answer." Temple slammed down the phone.

"I'm calling the police," McCabe said heavily.

"No! Don't do anything hasty yet. I'm going down there. I can get a plane to Wichita around ten and rent a car there. I'll find out what this is all about and call you back." He whirled and galloped out of the office.

While he packed he carefully figured out all the reasons for the fantastic purchases and the sudden desperate need for money on the part of the Meteoritics Team. Once it was carefully analyzed, it all fitted together quite neatly.

Van Arden had been right. Those meteorites, maintaining their precise formation, had been just what he suspected—controlled vehicles. Inside were emissaries from some far world in space, paying their first

20

visit to Earth. Naturally, they were totally alien and no matter what their peaceful intent, they would frighten most of the population.

Therefore, the team would make every effort to keep the discovery secret until they had thrown up proper safeguards to protect not only the visitors but terrestrials. Temple, who got a secret kick out of science fiction, began to visualize a delegation of radioactive pollywogs or super-intelligent octopods.

In the midst of this relaxing reverie he caught sight of his wildly distracted face in the mirror, glared at it, and snarled, "Who the hell do you think you're kidding, you stupid jerk?"

His telephone rang. The voice was that of Mullane, but it had a curiously flat tone, as if being rebroadcast. "Curt, I know how anxious you are to visit the meteorite fall and to see Lee Mason. I have just been invited to rush down there for some special research. A car is here, waiting to take me, and since this is the weekend with no classes for two days it occurred to me that you might like to go along for a visit. You can fly back for Monday."

"Mulley," Temple shouted. "I'm all packed to catch a plane down, but of course I'd rather ride with you. But what's going on down there, anyhow? Who called you? What kind of special research? Did you talk to Lee? Is everyone all right?"

"Whoa, boy," Mullane broke in. "Take it easy. We've got a long ride ahead, with plenty of time for me to explain everything on the way. Hold your fire and we'll pick you up in ten minutes."

Temple was pacing nervously in front of his apartment building when a black sedan with Kansas license plates rounded the corner. He grabbed his suitcase and sprinted to meet it. The driver was a gaunt, weather-beaten man. A younger counterpart sat beside him. They both stared at him with curious, fixed intensity as Mullane, alone in the back seat, swung the door open.

"Get in, Curt. These are the Solles, father and son, who are doing so much to advance our work."

The two continued to stare without speaking as Temple acknowledged the odd introduction and ducked his head to climb in. At that moment something that felt like an icicle with legs hit the back of his neck. Halfway into the car, Temple brushed at it, feeling nothing but the ridges of scar tissue under his hair. The sensation went away. Young Solle twisted around.

"Not this one," he cried. "Oh, no! Not this one at all."

Mullane bent forward, his face twisted. "We've made a mistake, Curtis. A terrible mistake. We can't take you with us after all. Get out quickly and forget the whole thing."

"The hell I will," Temple yelled. "Are you off your rocker, Mully?

21

I'm not budging until you tell me what this is all about. Are you being kidnapped?"

He lunged inward and young Gus Solle leaned back to slug him on the cheekbone with a fist that felt like a sack full of scrap iron. Temple was doubled over and off balance, with one foot in the car and the other just lifting from the curb, his right hand occupied with maneuvering his suitcase in.

The blow knocked him back onto the rear seat. He scrabbled wildly to recover his balance, his eyes full of tears and whizzing meteors. Mullane grabbed his shoulders with surprising strength and heaved. Temple flew backward out of the car, still clutching the suitcase, and landed on his back on the grass with an impact that drove the breath from his lungs.

The door slammed and the car took off with a roar. It took the corner with a squeal of tortured rubber and was gone before he could get his breath and climb to his feet. He stood, panting, shaking. There was a sharp, throbbing pain at the back of his skull and he knew a moment's panic at the possibility that the impact had undone all the doctor's fine work.

There was nothing he could do about it now. He stumbled back into his apartment, phoned the airport for a reservation and ordered a rental car to be ready at Wichita. A gentle probing at the back of his head found considerable soreness but no evidence of deeper injury.

He gulped aspirins for the headache and examined himself in the mirror. It was something of a shock. Besides dirt, grass stains and general dishevelment, there was a darkening bruise on his right cheekbone and a wild glare in his eyes that added nothing to his looks.

He washed, changed clothes and belted down a therapeutic slug of bourbon. By the time the airport limousine came for him, both the glare and the headache had subsided considerably and he was fairly calm. It was a calm born more of numbness than control, but at least he looked fairly presentable, except for the bruise, and that he could do nothing about.

* * * *

The first streaks of dawn were paling the eastern sky when Curtis Temple pulled up at an all-night diner and gas station on the fringe of a town. He hated to stop, even for minutes, but sheer exhaustion was proving stronger than his desperation. Several times he had caught himself on the verge of falling asleep at the wheel of his rented car.

While a pimply-faced attendant serviced the car, he stumbled wearily into the diner and order black coffee. "How much further is it to

Bomer?"

The counterman eyed him suspiciously and finally decided he was not being kidded. "You're in it, mister—what there is of it."

Temple stared at him blearily while the words filtered into his consciousness. For the past couple of hours he had driven in such a daze of exhaustion that he had lost track of miles. He blinked. "I'm looking for the Solle farm."

"That figures," the counterman said. "That's where everybody's headed these days. Just stay on the highway for another twenty miles and watch for Gus' mailbox on your right."

A slim man in the uniform of a state trooper had come from the washroom, massaging his hands, and taken a stool down the counter where a cup of pale coffee and two greasy-looking doughnuts waited. He studied Temple in the mirror, then swung around. "You a reporter?"

Temple shook his head and tested his coffee. It was still too hot.

"You won't need the mailbox," the trooper said, through a mouthful of doughnut. "If it's still dark, you can see their floodlights for miles. If it's light, you can see their tower almost as far."

Temple set his coffee down so abruptly that it slopped over into the saucer. He stared at the trooper. "Did you say *tower*?"

"Regular skyscraper," the counterman contributed. "Clear up to hell and gone into the air, and not a window in it. Nobody can figure out what those eggheads are up to, but they're spending money like it was going out of style. If you ask me, that's gonna turn out to be another Cape Canaveral."

Temple abruptly stood up, threw a quarter on the counter and started for the door. The trooper swung around on his stool. "Just a minute. If you're figuring to go out there for a look, you can save time and gas. Sightseers aren't allowed out there any more. They've got an electrified fence around the whole layout and armed guards to run off anybody who tries to snoop or hang around."

"Thanks," Temple said through his teeth and started on.

The trooper came off his stool with a rush. "Hold it, you! I think I'd like to know who you are and what your business is with that bunch out there. Let's see your driver's license."

Temple fought down a surge of anger and got out his wallet with his license and several other identification cards in the transparent pockets. "I didn't know Kansas had turned into a police state."

"It just got that way, Doc," the trooper said, studying the cards, "when some birds like you took over Solle's farm and started pulling some very funny shenanigans."

It was growing harder for Temple to suppress the anger.

"Shenanigans such as putting up a fence to keep rubbernecks from

23

trampling over and interfering with vital research?"

"That and other things. Like putting some kind of hex on Gus Solle so he draws out all his savings and mortgages his farm clear to the hilt. Like making the Solles and a lot of others around here act like some kind of zombies. My Dad's president of the bank and he hasn't been himself since the day that blond witch from the camp talked him out of a whopping, unsecured loan."

Temple suppressed a start. He could only mean Lee Mason. The fear that had been growing inside him swelled until it absorbed all other emotions.

"It must be legal, because our headquarters got word right from Washington to mind our own business and keep hands off. We have to take it, but we don't have to like it." He slapped the wallet into Temple's hand. "Go ahead, Doc. But you won't mind if I ride along behind, just to make sure you don't get lost on the way."

CHAPTER 5

Armed Camp

Even in the gray half-light of morning, Temple could see the glow of powerful floodlamps from several miles away. By the time he turned off the highway he could make out the dark shape of the tower, rearing a good three hundred feet into the sky. He caught his breath, his brain reeling with the effort of trying to associate it, or anything else he had learned so far, with the original meteorite project.

In the rearview mirror he saw that the police car was no longer following but had parked on the highway shoulder, near the Solle mailbox. The trooper had climbed out and was standing behind it, watching him.

The rutted, unpaved country road topped a small rise in the rolling prairie land. Temple sucked in his breath sharply. Nothing had quite prepared him for the sight ahead.

Rising out of the parched land was virtually a small city. Its heart and center was the weird tower looming skyward, capped by a network of uncovered beams and girders over which a horde of workmen swarmed like ants. The turquoise brilliance of acetylene torches winked on and off like fireflies, and the dawn wind brought the faint clatter of riveting hammers.

Around the base of the tower were open lots piled high with lumber, girders and what seemed to be sheets of steel. Outside this circle were buildings of various sizes. Some were still under construction, revealing a flimsy frame and tar paper basis to account for the speed with which the complex had gone up.

A lump rose in Temple's throat as he spied the familiar prefab huts of the original meteor camp tucked off to one side, dwarfed by the huge new structures. They looked forlorn and forgotten, as forgotten as Curtis Temple who had created them.

But the most obvious item of all was the fence, glinting like polished silver in the first rays of the rising sun. A full ten feet high, it surrounded the entire complex, including the weathered, unpainted buildings of the original Solle farm. The only visible gate was the one barring the road a half-mile or so ahead.

Temple had halted the car on the crest. As he sat gaping at the incredible scene, his ears caught a faint, throbbing rumble that grew steadily louder. Suddenly it was overhead and, leaning out, he saw a large multi-passenger helicopter bearing the orange-red markings of the Air Force. It swept by, made a wide circle and drifted down out of his sight to a landing behind the Solle barn.

"I'll be damned!" Temple whispered aloud. He reached for the automatic transmission lever and saw that his hand was shaking violently.

He got himself under control and drove on, stopping a few yards from the massive gate. At intervals along the fence he saw big red-lettered signs reading:

WARNING !
DANGER—CHARGED FENCE
10,000 VOLTS
TO TOUCH OR APPROACH CAN BE FATAL

At the approach of the car, a beefy, hard-faced man with a revolver holstered from his belt ran from a small guard shanty inside the gate. He raced to the road, well back of the gate, waving powerful arms and bawling something.

Temple ignored him until he had made a closer inspection of the fence and the layout beyond. As far as he could see into the camp, a veritable army of workmen were sawing, hammering, lugging or dashing about, in and out of the buildings. Everything they did was at a frenzied speed that reminded him sharply of the old-time movies.

The gate guard was still yelling hoarsely when Temple finally got out, leaving the motor idling. His eyes were glittering slits in the taut gray mask of his face. He tramped purposefully toward the gate, clenched fists swinging loosely as his sides.

"Get back, you goddamn idiot!" the guard bawled, windmilling his arms violently. "Can't ya read? There's enough hot stuff in this gate to kill an elephant, and plenty of it leaks into the ground. Get back in that bus and clear out quick. This is private property. Nobody gets in and nobody's allowed to hang around outside. Now beat it, buddy."

"Shut up!" Temple said coldly. "Get on your phone in there and tell Miss Mason that Curtis Temple is out here. She'll see me."

The beefy man gave his pistol belt a hitch, spat into the dust and gave Temple a malevolent glare. "A hell of a lot you know about it, buddy. I've got news for you. My orders are not to bother Miss Mason or none of the others with calls like this when they're busy workin'. If you got sump'n important to say, write a letter. They might read it. So now, clear out, bud."

"Can't you even call them in case of an emergency?"

"It would have to be a pretty damn big emergency, I can tell you that. So—"

"It will be, my friend," Temple said gently.

He turned and tramped along the edge of the road until he saw fair-sized rock half-buried in the dry earth. He squatted down, worked his fingers around it and tugged, ignoring a profane yell from the guard. It came loose in his hands.

He smiled sweetly at the gaping guard, carried the rock over to the car and propped it on top of the accelerator. Under its weight the gas pedal went almost to the floor and the engine's murmur climbed to a shattering roar. Reaching in the open door, Temple took hold of the transmission lever.

He grinned at the slack-jawed guard and lifted his voice above the racket. "You'd better get back a little further, fellow. I wouldn't want you run over or electrocuted when my car smashes through your gate."

"*Wait*! Don't do it, for God's sakes! I'll phone Miss Mason. Just don't do no more damn fool tricks. I only work here."

He galloped for the guard shanty, throwing fearful glances over his shoulder. Temple waited grimly, letting the engine race and keeping a hand on the lever until the guard reappeared, nodding and mopping his red face. He leaned in and slid the rock off the accelerator, cutting the roar back to a murmur.

"She'll be right over, mister. You just wait and don't try no more screwy tricks."

Temple saw her then, hurrying along the camp street at the same accelerated tempo that seemed to mark everyone inside except the guard. His breath caught at the sight of her remembered loveliness.

Then, as she came closer, a wave of almost physical sickness knotted his middle. She was the same Lee Mason, yet not the same. It was not the cold anger on her face, nor anything else tangible he could put a finger on. All the perfection of line and color was there, yet something was lacking. It came to him that she resembled a beautiful wax doll, a perfect image of Lee Mason, yet without some vital inner spark. The words of the state trooper leaped into his mind: "like some kind of zombies." He tried to greet her, to call her name, but he could push no more than a wordless croak through the lump in his throat. She halted a few yards from the gate and stared at him with no trace of the warmth he remembered in her eyes.

"Why are you creating a disturbance out here, annoying all of us and interrupting our work? President McCabe gave you express orders not to come here at all, Curtis."

The rebuke was like a knife stab through his heart. "I had to come, to find out what happened to you. You suddenly stopped writing or

27

phoning, and when I couldn't get through to you I nearly went crazy. I happen to be in love with you, Lee."

"Sentiment," she said furiously. "I will not have it interfering with our vital work."

"What is this vital work, Lee? What kind of a mad tangent have you all gone off on? If I had some idea of what you're doing, I might be able to understand your strange actions, maybe even help you."

"You *can* help us, Curtis," she said earnestly. "You can help more than you know…by quietly going away and staying away. Don't come here again or try to contact or spy on any of us. When the proper time comes, you will understand. Until then, you are keeping me from my work. Good-bye, Curtis."

"Lee—" he cried, but the torrent of words died unshouted.

She turned her back and snapped her fingers at the guard. "If you ever see this man sneaking around or trying in any way to get inside or attract our attention, you are to deal with him as you would any other intruder. Is that clear?"

"Yes, *ma'am*!" He slapped the bolstered pistol and glared at Temple. "If he hadn't tried to ram the gate—"

"It won't happen again," Lee said flatly. "This afternoon there will be an outer barricade of slanting steel spikes installed across the road. No vehicle will be able to pass them until they are lowered from inside your guard shanty."

Temple watched her depart with that same automaton speed. Dull-eyed and heavy-hearted, he got into the car, turned around and headed back toward the highway, dropping the useless rock off beside the road. He almost wished now that he had made good his threat to crash the gate, though it would probably have gotten him shot. He had a sick feeling that the Lee Mason he had just listened to would order his execution without the slightest hesitation if he interfered with the mysterious "work."

That was not the Lee Mason he knew and loved, the girl who had worked with him in the laboratory and walked hand in hand with him under the stars. This was a totally alien creature, a lovely shell from which all human emotions had been drained.

How or why he could not even guess. Was she hypnotized, possessed, enslaved? He beat a clenched fist against the wheel and his jaw ached from the tension of clenched teeth. Whatever the answer was, he would find it and somehow bring back the spark of life to her eyes and the laughter to her voice.

Meanwhile, he was groping in total darkness without even an idea of where to start. He knew only one thing for certain: In order to save Lee Mason he would have to steel himself against emotions, become as cold and ruthless as she.

He was almost to the main highway when a man got up from a bank beside the road and stepped out, jerking his thumb in the traditional hitchhiker's gesture. Temple stepped on the brake, his interest quickening.

"Mind giving me a lift to town?"

Temple swung the door open. "Hop in. What are you doing afoot out here in the middle of nowhere?"

The stranger settled back and grinned. "Waiting for you, Doc." He was a large, rather nondescript man with pale brown eyes and pale brown hair. "You are Curtis Temple, aren't you?"

"How…"

"Cramer, that state trooper, told me about meeting you at the diner. In fact, he dropped me back there on Solle's road to wait for you. It was lucky for me your girl friend gave you the brush-off. If you'd gone through with that damn fool stunt of ramming the gate, I'd be facing a mighty long, hot walk about now."

The car slammed to a jolting stop and Temple glared at him wildly. "How do you know about all that? Who are you, anyhow?"

"Stilwell, FBI. As to knowing what went on…" He fished in a jacket pocket and produced a pair of compact folding binoculars. "These may look like toys but they help me do a pretty fair job of detecting at half a mile, Doc. Now, what say we find us a less conspicuous parking place and see if we can't horse-trade some information about things that are bugging us both?"

CHAPTER 6

The Crimson Plague

When he finally parked on a remote side road, Temple described everything that had occurred from the moment of Van Arden's call to the present; he explained the organization and purpose of the Meteoritics Team. He finished grimly, "The only thing I know for sure is that Lee Mason is not herself in any way. I don't know about the rest of..."

"The same," Still said gloomily. "But there's nothing you can pin down. It's like wrestling a patch of fog. I'm not supposed to be on this case because officially there isn't any case. They haven't busted any laws that I know of. If they've bent any, it was with official sanction."

"I can swear Mullane was kidnapped. He wouldn't act as he did of his own free will. I know him well enough to know that."

"You'd play hell making it stick," Stilwell said wearily. "They arrived just ahead of you this morning with Mullane driving and both Solles sound asleep in the back. That makes nine top scientists in three days who have come under their own power and apparently of their own volition. I'd bet that Air Force chopper you saw brought more of them."

"Then why are you spying on them?" Temple demanded. Stilwell scowled. "It started the night those fireballs appeared and all hell broke loose in Washington. Van Arden couldn't decide whether he thought they were missiles or space ships full of purple people eaters, so he hedged his bets. He called out your team in case they came from space, and mine—along with the CIA—in case they came from behind the Curtain. Those first few days, I got pretty well acquainted with both Van and your people and I liked them all. Then suddenly I didn't like them at all." Temple swung sharply, his eyes narrow. "Go ahead."

"Everybody was laughing and excited the night they hauled those rocks out and cracked them open. Half an hour later they were all like your girl friend, like zombies. Van Arden put in a call to Washington and talked almost an hour. I don't know who he called or what he said, but about midnight every one of us outside your science team got orders to pull out and keep hands off. Something didn't smell right to me at all, so I thought up a couple of excuses to hang around Bomer. But for all I've learned since, I might as well be back in Wichita running my field office."

"But there must be a thousand workmen in there," Temple said.

"And all the material for that layout. They didn't just pull that out of thin air."

"Not quite, but almost. The Mason girl visited local lumber and building supply men, they started phoning and for forty-eight hours every road in this end of the state was choked with trucks. She called on the local employment agency and workmen started arriving by plane, train and bus. They're getting fantastic wages but that's all I know. Not one's been permitted to set foot outside that fence since he was hired. You may not like this, Doc, but it looks very much as if your blonde is the boss of the whole show. Everyone she's called on has shut up like a clam and acted like a zombie ever since."

Temple's clenched fists hammered against the wheel in helpless frustration. Suddenly he whirled, his eyes alight. "Somebody high up in Washington is making all this possible. That person must know what it's all about. Haven't you any contacts in the Bureau or around the Pentagon who might leak?"

Stilwell's jaw set. "I just might. Doc. Come to think of it, I just might. I'm probably asking him to lay his neck on a block and holler for the axe, but damn it, this is no time to be squeamish. Let's go put in a call and blast the poor guy's career all to hell."

On the main street of Bomer, Stilwell pointed to a sign bearing the familiar white bell on blue background. "There's the local telephone office. Park as close as you can and I'll put in my call from there. They know me so we can get some privacy."

Temple found a parking space and started around the car to join the FBI man on the sidewalk. Stilwell started to say something but his voice broke on a strangled cry. An expression of fearful agony twisted his face. His big body stiffened and went up on tiptoe as if every joint had locked under some intolerable tension. Several passers-by stopped, gaping. Temple lunged forward with outstretched hands.

Suddenly it appeared as if some terrible internal pressure exploded, forcing every drop of blood in Stilwell's body out to the surface. His pale brown eyes bulged into glassy protrusions. The flesh of his face and neck puffed out and turned a bright, ugly crimson, dotted with droplets of exuded blood that gave it the appearance of raw beef.

For an instant Stilwell poised on his toes, then plunged forward. Temple caught the plunging body and lowered it, stiff as a statue, to the sidewalk. He was stunned by the suddenness and horror of the seizure, only dimly aware that somewhere close by a woman was shrieking and a babbling crowd was closing in.

A man fought his way through, shouting, "I'm a doctor. Let me through here. Get out of the way." He knelt by Temple, cried, "Good

God!" and snatched a stethoscope from the bag he carried. After a moment he straightened, shaking his head. "Whatever it is, he's beyond help now."

No one thought of contagion. To the pushing crowd it was only a strange and morbidly fascinating form of death. Half a dozen willing volunteers crowded in to help carry Stilwell's body across to the funeral establishment that also served as local morgue. As they picked it up, a sudden impulse made Temple slip the small, powerful binoculars from Stilwell's jacket pocket to his own.

He stood back in the white-tiled embalming room while the doctor completed a superficial examination of the body. Temple was still dazed by the swiftness of the tragedy, too shocked to realize the magnitude of his own loss.

The doctor straightened at last, shaking his head. "This beats me. I've never encountered or even read of anything remotely resembling these symptoms. Before we do another thing, I'm going to phone the State Medical Association and ask for instructions. We may be facing a rare or wholly new form of disease."

He looked almost happy about it as he reached for the telephone. The next moment he was stiffening, crashing to the floor, his face masked by the same hideous suffusion of blood.

The men who had been lingering surreptitiously after carrying Stilwell's body in stared for a moment in pop-eyed horror. Then with yells of terror, they whirled and ran, jamming the doorway with a clawing, howling mass. On the sidewalk outside, a huge crowd had gathered, waiting for further news of the mysterious malady. The panic-stricken bearers burst out like a cork from a bottle, scattering those nearest the door.

The last man to emerge took two steps, stiffened and went down with a blood mask for a face. As the crowd broke into a screaming bedlam, another of the volunteer pallbearers was felled in their midst. By the time Curtis Temple reached the sidewalk, the fear-maddened mob was in full flight, jamming the street in both directions. In the immediate area there was no one but the two grotesque bodies on the sidewalk.

Moving like a man in a nightmare, and with no clear motivation, Temple got the first victim under the armpits and began to drag the stiff figure toward the mortuary door. Suddenly the funeral director, a plump little man with snow-white hair, ran out and lifted the feet.

He looked at Temple with frightened eyes and said, "Somebody has to do it, and I've already handled the first one enough to catch it if I'm going to."

By the time they had laid the two bodies beside that of the doctor

32

on the morgue room floor, other courageous townspeople were coming in quietly to help do what must be done. Doctors contacted state and national medical authorities. A reporter put the story on the press wires, then went on the air to plead for calm. Cramer set up highway patrol roadblocks to turn travelers away from the stricken town. Police and businessmen patrolled streets to avert mass panic.

Because they had already been exposed, Temple and Adams, the mortician, took over the job of moving the bodies to an empty shed out beyond the edge of town. They used the hearse and left it at the shed, plodding back on foot in numb silence.

No more victims were stricken that night. By morning the vanguard of an army of medical warriors began arriving to battle the horrible disease. An emergency laboratory was set up and squads moved out to find the enemy, grimly analyzing soil, water, air, food, anything that might conceivably have bred contagion or carried it in.

On their heels came some of the country's leading medical authorities with a team of courageous nurses. A warehouse at the edge of town was converted into a pathology center where they began the grisly task of autopsying the bodies of the victims and subjecting organs and tissues to every known test.

As the day wore on with no new cases, a measure of calm returned to the town and bolder citizens began to resume their normal activities. But within the ranks of the searchers there was no calm but a growing dismay.

By mid-afternoon they faced the incredible fact that nowhere was there a clue to the mystery malady. No contamination of any sort could be found in the area. The bodies showed no unfamiliar virus or bacteria, no trace of any organic malfunction to explain the seizures. Teams of researchers, digging into the vast treasury of medical experience, found no record of any case even remotely similar anywhere in the world.

The doctors, equipped with every modern defense against contagion, took complete charge of burying the remains of the victims in a remote area far from town. Within an hour after that task was completed, three doctors, a nurse, the workmen who had volunteered to fill the graves and an innocent farmer two miles from the site were stricken with a return of what newspapers and television had christened "The Crimson Plague."

A fresh panic rolled out in waves to engulf the country. In Topeka the Governor declared a state of emergency. National Guard units were flung completely around Bomer in a wide, tight cordon to prevent anyone's leaving town and thereby possibly spreading the unknown contagion.

Temple, reeling with exhaustion, had finally been forced to take a

33

hotel room and sleep a few hours. When he returned to emergency headquarters to give whatever aid he could, his mind was still too numb to think beyond the moment or to wonder how he had so far escaped the Crimson Plague.

The bodies of the latest victims had been stored in the same shed Temple and Adams had used for the first victims. Shortly after dark a grim and silent mob marched out from town. Temple followed them, mystified but unable to get a word of explanation from those he tried to question. Near the shed the main body halted.

A dozen or so men went on and, from a cautious distance, hurled buckets of gasoline over the shed and the hearse parked beside it. Others moved up to throw burning torches. In a moment both shed and hearse were a mass of roaring flames. The mob stood watching in ominous and frightening silence as the fire completed its work of total destruction. With the collapse of the last shed wall, the silent crowd began to turn away, its macabre effort at self-preservation completed.

A sudden gust of night wind came out of the west, causing the flames to dance eerily, lifting a swirl of ashes from the ruins. The soft flakes swept down over the crowd and almost instantly people began dropping with the unmistakable symptoms of the Crimson Plague.

Curtis Temple could only stand frozen as the survivors, half mad with terror, fled screaming back across the prairie to town. Behind them, more than a score of bodies lay stiff and lifeless on the ground.

In the small hours of morning a group of the nation's leading medical authorities faced one another grimly, after hours of secret discussion. The chairman rose, his face gray, his eyes dull with despair.

"I don't have to remind you, gentlemen, that not a word or hint of what has been said here tonight must pass these doors. I'm afraid the public at large will learn the truth soon enough. We have reached agreement on only one point—we are completely and hopelessly stumped. The Crimson Plague cannot be either anticipated or checked by any means at our command. Neither burial nor cremation appear to destroy its virulence or hamper its spread. We don't know what it is, where it came from or how to halt it."

One of his distinguished colleagues lifted a haggard face. "We know one more fact. Unless we find some place where the bodies of Crimson Plague victims can be isolated beyond all possibility of even remote contact with the living, the contagion may quickly spread over the nation and then the entire globe."

CHAPTER 7

Sinister Fortress

In his hotel room Temple paced the floor, beating clenched fists together in an agony of frustration. The television screen in one corner of his room showed a long aerial view of Bomer, taken from a distance of several miles and including part of the ring of Guardsmen. An announcer whose voice trembled on the verge of hysteria was urging the public to remain calm.

During the early hours of morning the Crimson Plague had leaped the human barricade surrounding Bomer and struck simultaneously at a score of towns within a radius of sixty miles. So widely separated were the stricken areas that it was impossible to blame the spread on a frightened refugee who might have slipped through the cordon carrying infection.

It was fearfully obvious that the Plague moved and spread by a means of its own, independent of human carriers. If this were so, then man's sole, feeble hope of confining and controlling it was gone. A famous commentator, better known for sensationalism than sense, added to the frenzy by coining the phrase, "Today Kansas—Tomorrow The World!" Others hinted darkly at germ-warfare experiments behind the Iron Curtain.

Temple snapped off the set and stood gritting his teeth in impotent despair. His casual phrase, *The Gods Hate Kansas*, suddenly took on new and sinister meaning.

The meteorites had fallen on Kansas. The fantastic change in the personalities of the Meteoritics Team had occurred there. Now, from that same focal point, the Crimson Plague was spreading its deadly tentacles. It was impossible to see all this as mere coincidence. The mysteries had to be linked somehow into a single dark pattern.

Why hadn't he himself caught the Plague if it were so contagious? He had been in closest contact with Stilwell both before and after his death. Were deadly, undiscoverable organisms already incubating in his own bloodstream, awaiting their time to strike? But others had escaped equal or even greater exposure. Was there any relationship between the meteorites, the Crimson Plague and the strange activities of the meteor camp?

His spinning thoughts persisted in returning to Stilwell's death. Was his selection as the first victim of the horror no more than random chance? The FBI man had shared Temple's suspicions and had willingly become his ally in probing the mysteries. He had been on the verge of a phone call that promised the first tangible clue.

Temple had no idea of whom he had been about to call, or even in what branch of the government. That avenue had been effectively blocked by Stilwell's death. Was it coincidence or sinister design? If design, why had Temple been spared to continue his own determined probe of the mysteries?

The endless chain of unanswered questions blurred in his throbbing head. Out of the chaos, only one clear fact emerged. The answer to all the questions lay behind the electrified fence that guarded the camp. Until he could pass that barrier and get inside, all speculation was fruitless and pointless. There had to be a way into the camp, and he must find it quickly.

The determination steadied him and brought back the steely glint to his eyes. He swallowed pills for the headache, went out into the morning heat and stood looking up and down the street. The sign he was looking for caught his eye.

The Bomer Employment Agency was a narrow office with two empty desks behind a railing and a small closed room at the rear. A bell jangled as Temple walked in and a man came from the small room. He was thin, with an expressionless face and empty eyes that reminded Temple sharply of Lee Mason's.

"I understand they're hiring electricians out at that meteorite camp," Temple began. "I—"

"Not any more," the thin man interrupted. "Jobs are filled."

"Maybe I could leave an application anyhow, in case one gets hurt or sick and they need a replacement."

"They won't," the other said flatly. "The work's about finished. Sorry." He terminated the conversation by walking off.

Temple left, looking thoughtful. He spent the next few hours tramping the streets, pumping storekeepers or anyone else who had contact with the camp. The results were disheartening. None had ever made deliveries to the camp. No one from there came to town except Lee Mason, or one of the Solles who picked up grocery orders.

"You won't get anything out of Gus or his boy," the grocer told him. "They never was much for talking, but now they act like they're walking in their sleep. You ask 'em something, they just stare into space and don't hear you."

Temple's last call was on the electrical wholesaler who had furnished the equipment and materials. A list of what had been bought might give him a clue to the nature of the mysterious activity going on inside the camp.

The wholesaler was affable enough until Temple asked about the purchases. Then his face went blank. He stared with empty eyes and muttered vaguely, "They bought a lot of stuff. I don't remember what all it was."

"You must have records, invoices, purchase orders," Temple persisted. "Was most of it big, heavy equipment, or delicate instruments?"

"I...can't seem to remember. Somebody—that blond girl—took all the records to check. I must get them back sometime."

Temple gave up and left, the bitter taste of defeat in his mouth. There was no doubt that, somehow, the dealer had been thoroughly brain-conditioned, all knowledge of his transactions with the Meteoritics Team erased from his mind.

The sun was setting when he got his car and drove out to the Solle place. In that flat, treeless country there was no place of concealment. Below the last rise he pulled off onto the prairie a hundred feet or so from the lane and hoped that it would be unnoticed in the deepening gloom.

He climbed to the crest and looked down upon the camp. The floodlights were blazing and the whole place seethed with the same frenzied activity. The tower was now capped by a domed roof and most of the smaller buildings seemed to be finished on the outside. Somewhere heavy machinery snorted and rumbled and hammers thudded. From open doors came the purple glare and fitful *spat* of arc welders. Stilwell's powerful binoculars brought the scene closer but added no details of significance.

They did show him that Lee had made good her threat. Across the road in front of the gate stretched a barricade of steel teeth, sharp-pointed and slanting outward from a serrated bed into which they could fold to let a car pass. A new rough-board structure stood a few yards outside the gate. This was simply a roof and back wall covering a long bench. It resembled the shelters often erected at bus stops, but its purpose here baffled him.

When full darkness had fallen, Temple moved down as close to the fence as he could without being caught in the backwash of lights. From this close range, the activity inside seemed even more frenetic and less comprehensible. He was suddenly struck by the absence of human voices, the bawling of orders and requests, the noisy banter that usually emanated from a work crew. Here, it was like watching voiceless robots dashing about. The discovery brought an eerie prickle to the back of his neck.

Moving warily away from the gate he found himself looking through the mesh fence into the original meteoritics camp, tiny and almost lost in a remote corner of the vast complex. No one moved outside

37

but there were lights shining from the windows of the huts and the larger laboratory. The sight brought a lump to his throat.

Then he saw the nine meteorites, lying on a platform beside the laboratory. Through the glasses he could make out the odd, pitchlike surface, but it had a dull, dusty look. Suddenly he knew with almost clairvoyant certainty that those mysterious visitors from space had lain there, untouched and forgotten, since the night they were dragged from their pits. The feeling only intensified the dark mystery and spurred his determination to get beyond that lethal barricade that guarded it.

He moved on, his hopes rising as he saw no signs of guards anywhere along the fence. Apparently they were depending upon high tension current alone for their security, and there were always ways to thwart man-made electricity. He studied the fence, his mind racing.

The steel posts of the fence were set into heavy insulators. An intruder touching the fence would become the conductor that carried the charge from the steel mesh to the ground. With thick rubber boots and the kind of insulating gloves worn by high-line crews he should be safe. It might even be possible to lean a heavily-insulated ladder against the fence without danger.

He stood there, visualizing the equipment he would need for the attempt when Fate in the form of a Kansas jack-rabbit intervened to save him from a fatal blunder. The rabbit, as large as a small dog, came bounding out of the night, perhaps chased by a hungry coyote or irresistibly drawn by the lights. It flashed by Temple in great six-foot leaps, sprang again and rammed headlong into the fence.

The gray body was a full three feet above the ground when it struck the mesh, but there was a blinding flash of sparks, a loud crackle and the stench of burned hair and flesh. Instantly, warning bells set up an ear-splitting clangor, and a signal light above that section of fence began to flash. A dozen guards with shotguns burst into sight, racing toward the indicated spot. Temple faded back into the night and ran.

He was still shaking when he reached his car. But for the rabbit, he would have gone ahead with a suicidal plan. Instead of being grounded to the earth, both poles of the current were in the mesh itself. However well insulated he might be from the soil, a touch would still be fatal and, judging by the arc, the potential was high enough to smash through insulating gloves. Furthermore, he had no doubt that simply touching the fence would set off the alarm bells and light.

The electrocution of the rabbit filled him with a sick horror. It emphasized more sharply than any other incident, the terrible change in Lee and the other team members. Instead of a jackrabbit, it could have easily been some person, innocently curious, who touched the fence. The callous indifference to human lives exemplified in that steel-mesh death trap was almost beyond comprehension.

He spent most of the night pacing the floor of his room, driving his numbed brain to find an answer to the dark mystery. In a corner the television kept up a low yammering. He listened with part of his mind on the slim chance that somewhere in the news there might be a clue. The Crimson Plague was spreading in the same crazy hit-and-miss pattern, flaunting puny medical barriers as arrogantly as it flaunted the laws of contagion. Its toll had reached past a thousand and was rising more swiftly.

About dawn he fell into a troubled sleep, only to be awakened almost immediately by a tumult from the street. From the window he saw the familiar Culwain trucks unloading a horde of workmen, mainly carpenters, judging by the tools they carried.

By the time he could throw on his clothes and get downstairs, the trucks were gone and most of the men dispersing to their homes. A number, however, were turning into an all-night restaurant down the street and he ran toward it, driven by new hope.

A half-hour later he stumbled out again, haggard and despondent. The carpenters had followed blueprints to build the flimsy structures that might, for all they knew or cared, have been hencoops. They were fed well, paid extravagantly and hustled back and forth from bunkhouses to job sites with no time to sightsee. Electricians, plumbers and steelworkers had followed the same pattern. No one explained or answered questions. They were all driven hard but paid well. Beyond that, they knew nothing of what was going on or what purpose their labor fulfilled.

He spent most of the day running down discharged workmen and getting the same answers. Only a handful, chiefly master electricians and welders, turned sullen and evasive under questioning. Temple finally gave up, convinced that they were more confused than hostile, simply because they could not remember what they had worked on. He was positive that like the employment agent and the electrical supplier, any significant memories of their activity within the camp had been erased from their minds.

He paced the streets, his steps timed to the rhythm of a refrain that beat against his frozen brain. *Get inside the camp! Get inside the camp!* The demand was an obsession that drove and ruled him. He ate little, slept less, grew steadily more gaunt and haggard. What was Lee doing in there, or what were they doing to her? Was there any hope that a spark of feeling for him still lingered in her heart? Had her true personality been ruthlessly destroyed or did it still lie imprisoned, waiting for him to break the chains that bound it?

Get inside the camp, his whole being cried. *Get inside and find out.*

39

The answers are all in there.

They were days of anguish for Curtis Temple. He made and aban-
doned a hundred wild and reckless plans. He spent long hours lying on
the hill, watching the camp through the glasses. Several times he saw
Lee and the others rushing from one building to another on mysterious
errands. Most of the activity now seemed to be centered in the great
central tower.

There were still several hundred workmen inside, mainly metal-
workers. Machines and human muscle were busy rushing sheet steel
and beams into the tower from the dwindling piles outside.

He quickly discovered the purpose of the covered bench outside.
Massive trailer trucks were bringing in loads of cable and pipe and
sheet metal now, along with what seemed to be enormous pieces of
machinery swathed in concealing tarpaulins. At the gate, the truck
driver got down and waited in the shelter while someone from inside
drove his truck through to the unloading point, then returned it empty.

Each time, before passing the gate, a team of armed guards
searched every inch of truck and load. The thoroughness of their inspection discouraged Temple from attempting to slip in as a stowaway.
He had a grim feeling that discovery would be highly unpleasant, if not
fatal. Twice he had been seen and shot at by the guards, with an accu-
racy that was unnerving.

He spent most of the nights battering his bloody head against the
apparently impregnable barrier of the fence. He hurled chains and
lengths of pipe against the fence, hoping to short-circuit and blow out
the system. Each time the alarm brought guards who cut out that section
of fence for the moments needed to remove the object.

He nursed an idea of bringing his car around over the prairie and
using it to smash down some remote section of the fence. That hope
died when, prowling in search of the best spot, he discovered a line of
sharpened stakes just far enough out from the fence to block such an
attempt.

The next night he brought a shovel with the hope of tunneling under
the fence. Before he had taken out a half-dozen shovelfuls, he felt the
sharp tingling in his hands and feet and remembered the gate guard's
warning of high tension leakage into the earth. If he could feel it on a
wooden shovel handle many yards away, the potential directly under
the fence would be enough to paralyze if not kill him. Again he gave
up in despair.

Day and night he continued fruitless efforts to reach Lee or any of
the others by telephone. The gravel-voiced Mrs. Solle always answered
and cut him off. He tried every subterfuge he could think of but she
displayed an uncanny skill in seeing through them all.

The thirteenth day after his frustrating talk with Lee Mason he saw a fresh burst of activity seize the camp. All day he lay on the ridge, watching bundles being carried into the tower in frantic haste. When nightfall brought no letup in the rush, he stayed at his post, watching through the glasses.

At last he saw the work crews being marched out and away to a building he had guessed were living quarters. When they were all inside, the floodlight suddenly blinked out, leaving the entire camp lit only by dim street lamps. He tensed with a feeling that events of vast importance were impending.

The light-gathering power of the glasses gave him a fairly good view despite the gloom. For some time nothing seemed to be happening. Then, as he swept the skyline of the camp, his breath caught sharply.

At the top of the tower the great dome was moving, splitting apart across the center. As he gaped, the two halves folded out and down, leaving the entire top open to the sky. In the space thus exposed he could make out the shadowy shape of a bluntly rounded nose protruding above the tower wall.

He scrambled to his feet, spurred by a stab of unreasoning terror, not for himself but for Lee and those others inside. An incoherent yell burst from his lips, although the conscious part of his mind was still numb to the realization of what he was seeing.

Then he became aware of a rumbling mutter, so low on the tonal scale that he felt it as vibration rather than heard it as sound. Under his feet the ground quivered. The mutter climbed to a full-throated bellow and the violent rocking of the earth dislodged rocks from the slope of the ridge. At the top of the tower a faint glow of light illuminated the protruding nose. Then light and sound rose together to furious crescendo.

His eardrums ached to sound and pressure. A blinding white light blossomed, turning the night into day. Then, through the brilliance, a dark and gleaming cylinder belched from the open maw of the tower and crept up with accelerating fury.

Temple stood frozen, transfixed. Once, with a group of invited scientists, he had watched a rocket launching at Cape Canaveral. This was like that, and yet different.

The great vehicle itself was similar but there was no cloud of vapor, no boiling backlash of flame. Instead, there was only a slim column of dazzling white stretching from the cylinder down into the tower, as if the rocket were being pushed up by a piston of molten metal rigidly confined within a cylinder of glass.

Instinctively he pressed a stud on the edge of his wrist watch. His

41

eyes never left the rocket, mounting with incredible speed, dragging the white tail up with it into the sky.

Abruptly the tail vanished. For another second or two the rocket was a pinpoint spark moving among the stars. Then there was a soundless flash and the spark was gone.

Seconds later something that felt like a wave of high tension electric current swept over him. His flesh crawled with a feeling of being brushed by invisible feathers. Then the sensation was gone and he could feel the hairs of his skin flatten.

A rocket had gone up from an impossible launching pad within that tower. It had climbed, then vanished in a wisp of light. Had it blown itself up through a malfunction? Were there passengers aboard?

He waited for the sound of a blast to reach his ears but no sound came. When he was sure none would come, he whirled and raced toward his parked car with the blood pounding in his ears and a terrible anguish clawing at his nerves.

CHAPTER 8

Inside The Camp

Curtis Temple was an experienced and dedicated meteor-watcher. He had trained his eyes and muscles to the superb co-ordination essential to capturing every possible secret during the instant a flashing meteor was visible. It had become second nature for his subconscious to chart the fragmentary course of a vanishing spark across the pattern of stars and pure reflex for his finger to clock its speed on the special timer built into his wrist watch.

Heedless of spying eyes, he snapped on the dome light of the car and hunched under it with pad and pencil. His fingers flew through a maze of intricate calculations. Timing the spark across familiar asterisms, whose apparent diameter he knew, gave a fair approximation of the rocket's speed away from Earth. His knowledge of star positions behind it gave its angle of flight. A condensed pocket *Ephemeris* he always carried supplied the final figures.

He sat back, sucking in a deep, incredulous breath. A stop watch, a dying spark and mathematics had supplied one major answer to the mystery that had driven him frantic for two weeks. But in supplying it, new and more incredible mysteries had been revealed.

Unless his hurried calculations were far in error, a rocket had blasted off from the meteor camp at a trajectory and speed that would take it directly into the orbit of the moon. And the nine black meteorites whose arrival had set off this weird carnival of horror had apparently been launched *from* the moon.

It was clear now that the major activity of the meteor camp had been the construction of that rocket and its unorthodox launching pad within the tower. Skilled workmen had fabricated the vehicle itself inside the tower, only to have the memory of their incredible feat somehow erased.

The propulsion method was obviously far in advance of any being used on current space agency projects. Suddenly Temple remembered the identities of some of the scientists who had rushed to the camp after it was set up. Rayfield was a top authority on atomics, a member of the Atomic Energy Commission. Lanelle was the inventor of a new oxyllium explosive that showed promise of refinement into a rocket fuel. Mullane was an acknowledged world authority on selenography, the geography of the moon.

But why? Why? The question clawed at him. Why had such an accomplishment been kept secret and private? Had the meteorites revealed the presence on the moon of some treasure hoard so vast that lust for it had turned human beings into heartless machines?

A new thought brought pallor to his cheeks. Was the Crimson Plague behind the mystery? Had the little group foreseen the ultimate destruction of all mankind by the hideous disease and fled to some new world, leaving the old one to its doom? In the same breath he discarded the idea.

He had glimpsed enough of the ship to estimate its size. It could never, he was certain, transport twelve persons, even if a literal miracle had been performed in the matter of fuel and air supply. He was familiar enough with the problems of astrogation to feel certain it could not have carried more than two, or at most three, passengers.

Then that meant the others were still there in the camp, and in their hands still lay the key to the whole mystery. Suddenly the way into the camp burst upon him. It had been in front of him the whole time but only now, with his mind sharpened by the events of the past hour, did he see it.

He reached into the back seat and his hands closed on the chilled metal of a rifle barrel. A week before, after being shot at by the guards, he had stormed into town and bought a .30-30 with the crazy idea of shooting his way in. He had since cooled off but the rifle had lain where he dropped it in the back. Now he thanked his stars for that mad impulse. Tonight it would get him into the camp, but not in the manner he had first planned.

With the rifle beside him he started the car and headed up over the prairie swell, away from the road. He drove without his lights, guided by the faint radiance of the stars and trusting to luck not to hit a rock or pothole.

He halted at last, broadside to the fence and nearly half a mile east of the gate. He leaned the rifle against the fender, got the jack out of the trunk and walked toward the fence. The floodlights had not been turned back on and tonight they were essential to his plan.

Running through the darkness he hurled the jack against the fence. Crackling flame blazed from the impact, alarm bells set up their harsh clangor and the warning light began to flash. A moment later the floodlights came on, revealing the inevitable squad of guards racing toward the trouble spot.

Temple paused just long enough to locate his target, then turned and raced for the car. He heard the guards yell and a rifle *blammed*. The screech of the slug past his ear was close enough to indicate the miss was not deliberate. As he skidded around the front of the car, a shotgun bellowed and a storm of pellets rattled against metal and glass.

He snatched the rifle, laid it across the car's hood and let the sights come to rest on his target—the black mass of a power transformer on an elevated platform. He had noticed the transformer the first time he inspected the camp and recognized it as the nerve center of the deadly fence. But until tonight he had completely failed to realize its significance.

Now he lined the sights carefully and squeezed the trigger. The rifle bucked and thundered. There was a dull *clang* and the diminishing scream of a ricochet as the slug glanced off the rounded transformer shell. The charging guards were directly in the line of fire and the bullet whizzing overhead apparently convinced them they were under attack. As one they dropped to their knees to steady their aim and let go a thundering volley.

Buckshot and slugs slammed into the car, glanced off the hood and screeched past Temple's ears. Only the fact that he was in shadow beyond the light saved him.

Ignoring the deadly hail, he concentrated on putting his next shot dead center. The guards were barely a hundred yards away, shooting as they ran, when his second shot *blammed* out. A burst of livid flame and violet sparks engulfed the transformer and every light in the camp whipped out.

In the blinding darkness, he could hear the guards milling, colliding, cursing and yelling for flashlights. He ran along the fence until the noises were far behind, then hurled the rifle. It struck the mesh and slid down but there were no alarm bells, no blaze of high tension sparks. For the moment the barrier was dead. At any instant an emergency circuit might be cut in, restoring its murderous potential.

Temple shut his mind to that possibility, clawed his fingers into the steel network and went up like a squirrel, getting some added lift from his scrabbling toes. He reached the top and threw himself over and out into impenetrable blackness. Nothing he might land on could be more deadly than the fence reactivated.

He landed on all fours with a force that wrung a grunt of pain from him. He was instantly up and limping toward the black mass of buildings, driven by the desperate need to find cover before the lights came back on. Apparently the camp had not been prepared for the emergency his shot had created, or the bullet had done more damage to the power line itself than he anticipated.

Flashlights were weaving and bobbing from two directions as guards fanned out to cover the deadened fence. Temple dived into the blackness between two buildings and ran. His eyes were growing more accustomed to darkness so he could at least avoid major obstacles.

45

He burst out onto one of the camp streets. To his left were running figures with flashlights whipping their pale puddles from side to side. To his right the massive bulk of the rocket tower loomed and he ran toward it. In that monstrous cylinder lay the heart of the camp secrets.

Suddenly a dark shape sprang at him from the shadows of a row of parked trucks. He caught the glint of starlight on metal and heard the sharp inhalation of breath that proceeded a bellow of alarm. There was no time to identify the metal object or learn whether the figure was that of a guard or one of his own people.

Temple hurled himself at the figure, putting his full momentum behind a swinging fist. His knuckles met jawbone and pain lanced up his arm. The figure flew backward into a truck, rebounded and slammed to the ground. The glinting object rolled free and Temple snatched it, feeling the metal case of a flashlight.

He was almost to the tower when a flash beam swept out from behind a building, its puddle of light almost touching his feet. He swerved wildly and found cover behind some sort of crate as the bearer of the light stepped out. In the pale backwash of the light beam, he recognized the thin, ascetic face of Dr. Marko Spirovic, an authority on wave mechanics and one of the more recent arrivals at camp.

Temple held his breath while the sweeping light narrowly missed the figure of the man he had downed, then moved on. Flicking the beam from side to side, Spirovic moved past his hiding place and started on. Temple drew a soft breath of relief and started to creep on toward his goal.

He knew he had made no sound, but abruptly Spirovic swiveled around and pinned him unerringly with the flashlight beam. In its glow, Temple could see Spirovic's thin lips drawn back, giving his face a wolfish, predatory look. His left hand held the light while his right grabbed for a curious-looking gadget, somewhat resembling a camera flash gun, suspended from a shoulder strap.

What the thing was or how Spirovic had pinpointed his location so accurately were questions Temple left for later. He exploded from his crouch straight at the physicist. A wild yell burst from the slender figure as Temple's shoulder sent him rolling. There were answering cries from close by.

Temple stumbled, caught himself and ran. As he swerved to get off the open street, he saw Spirovic on his knees, pointing the strange object at him. A beam of ghostly bluish light shot from the flared barrel. Temple dodged instinctively and the beam only flicked one pistoning leg.

He felt an instant of searing agony. Then his leg went completely numb, throwing him forward onto hands and knees. The blue beam

46

snapped off and Spirovic ran toward him, shouting in a triumphant voice and tugging a flashlight from a hip pocket. For a fleeting moment Temple was in darkness.

His leg was a dead, useless thing, without life or feeling, but his other limbs seemed unaffected. Clawing at the ground, he scrabbled forward, dragging the paralyzed leg, hurling himself behind one of the parked trucks an instant before Spirovic's spare flashlight winked out.

Temple's ears were roaring, his lungs gasping for breath. Behind him lights were weaving and voices yelling, but below his thigh he could feel the first tingle of returning sensation in the numb leg. The touch of the ray, whatever it was, had apparently been too brief to hold long. He lurched to his feet and hobbled around the truck in a travesty of a run, stumbling and panting.

The pursuers momentarily lost him when he dived and rolled under a truck. He struggled up and ran again, limping and groaning, toward the tower. Behind him flashlights probed under and around the trucks.

Then clearly he heard Spirovic's heavily accented cry, "Over by the launch tower."

Temple swerved toward a low building against the tower's base, hands clawing at the knob of a door. It swung inward, strangely thick and ponderous, and he plunged forward into the inky darkness beyond. A blast of chill, dead air struck his face and he realized this was some kind of refrigerated storeroom for perishables. But it was at least a momentary hiding place, unless Spirovic was again guided by the uncanny faculty that had twice revealed itself.

He swung the door tight shut, turned and struck his feet on some solid but yielding object on the floor. He teetered, clawed at the empty darkness and fell with a jarring thud across whatever had tripped him. For a moment he lay still, fighting down the noisy gasping of starved lungs, listening for the faint sounds of the search outside. At best, he knew this haven was only temporary.

He braced his hands to lever himself up and felt cloth and a yielding firmness. A stab of alarm sent him rocking back from the thing beneath. He got the captured flashlight out of his pocket, shielded the lens with his jacket and snapped it on.

The dim glow of filtered radiance fell on the body of a man.

Temple rocked back on his heels, his breath wheezing loudly in the dead silence of the insulated cold room. Then there was no sound at all as the light touched the unmistakable bloated face of a Crimson Plague victim.

The light wavered, then steadied as he fought for a measure of self-control and won. The sound of his shallow breathing resumed. He forced himself to look more closely at the raw-beef face but there was

47

nothing recognizable. He lifted the light and gasped again, more sharply.

The whole far end of the room was filled with similar bodies, piled like cordwood to the ceiling.

His senses reeled and for a moment he teetered on the brink of madness. Somehow he had gained a belief that the people in the camp were immune to the Crimson Plague. But these victims must have been stricken inside the fence. But who were they? Workmen? Or were the bodies of his own team members in that gruesome stack? He realized with a sickening shock that some members of the Meteoritics Team had never appeared outside. Were his own close friends and associates here?

A terrible thought struck him. He had not seen Lee's golden hair among the crowds for at least two days. He started up suddenly, his jaw clenched against revulsion at the purpose forming in his mind.

The Plague so contorted features that it would be impossible to identify the average person. But Lee's blond hair would not be changed. He forced his dragging steps forward with a determination to examine every body in that pile to find her or reassure himself that she was not among the victims.

Behind him the heavy door swung open and a powerful light blazed in. The exultant voice of Spirovic cried, "You will not elude us again, Temple."

He was still swinging around to face them when the blue beam caught him full in the face. He knew a moment's blinding agony and then utter blackness.

CHAPTER 9

No Way Out

His eyes opened slowly and heavily. It seemed to take an eternity for them to focus and even longer for his sluggish senses to grasp the messages they sent.

He was lying on an iron cot in a small room without any other furniture and without windows. The only break in the four drab walls was a heavy wooden door. The ceiling was of stout steel mesh and the only light in the room came down through that from some artificial source outside his line of vision.

Then memory came back with a rush and he sat up, surprised to find that his hands and feet were free. Since there was nothing else to look at, he squinted up through the mesh ceiling and saw smooth, curving walls mounting up and up to an impossible height. At their top a vaulted roof seemed to have a crack that split it into two equal halves.

"The launch tower," he gasped aloud. "I'm in some kind of a prison cell at the base and looking up at that roof that opens to let the rocket out."

Then he remembered the cold room full of bodies and with it came the stabbing fear for the safety of Lee and the others. He sprang up and lunged against the door, only to find it rock-solid. The walls were as unyielding.

The low mesh ceiling caught his eye. He crouched, gathered himself and sprang straight up. His fingers clawed into the mesh, found holds and locked. He pulled himself up until his face was against the screen, immensely widening his angle of vision. His eyes snapped wide at the sight of the rocket ship almost filling the immense cylindrical silo.

It was much larger than it had seemed in flight, well over a hundred feet in length, covered with a dull, seamless metal skin in which no port was visible. Entrance, he guessed, must be through a port near the tail, well below his line of vision. The only visible feature was a cowling, like a fluted collar, that circled the hull below the bluntly rounded nose. From this cowling a ring of tubes flared back. He guessed they were steering and stabilizing jets of some sort.

By this time his straining muscles could take no more and he dropped back to the floor. His brain was spinning with new questions that could only be answered by someone behind this fantastic project.

He threw back his head, filled his lungs and let go a bellow that echoed and re-echoed from the distant dome.

"Hey!" he roared. "Get me out of here! What's the idea of locking me up?"

The booming echoes whispered away. He shouted again and again until his throat was raw and his lungs ached. When he had about given up in despair, he heard the pound of feet outside. A bolt slid aside with a rasping sound, and a sizable panel swung outward in the upper part of the door. Framed in the opening was the unsmiling face of Mullane.

"Curtis, I must insist that you stop creating a disturbance that seriously hampers our concentration. You were confined here because you persistently interrupted work of vital importance. When that work is completed you will be free to leave. In the meantime, if you will be quiet and orderly you will receive your meals on time and perhaps even a few books to read."

"To hell with books!" Temple yelled furiously. "And to hell with you, *old friend*! If I'm such a pest, why not just knock me in the head and shove me in that cold room with all the rest of stiffs?"

"We considered that," Mullane said coldly, "but concluded that this way presented less annoyance. I hope you won't force us to change our minds, Curtis."

Temple looked at the empty eyes and the expressionless face that belonged both to a warm friend and a cold stranger. His anger evaporated. "I'm sorry, Mully, but for God's sake can't you give me some idea of what's going on in here? I saw the Plague bodies piled up. Are any of them from the Meteoritics Team? Is Lee alive and well? Don't those bodies constitute a risk of contagion if you stay here?"

He could almost feel a relaxing of tension. Mullane's smile was almost human. "You can relax, Curtis. Lee is quite well and in no danger. She is—and all of us are—much too vital to the project to be permitted the slightest risk. Now I must return to my work." He started to close the panel.

"Wait," Temple cried. "You haven't told me anything about your work here. When did the rocket get back, or isn't this the one I saw take off?"

"It is the same one, Curtis. It returned on the following night, promptly on schedule."

"The following night? How long did that blue light keep me knocked out, and what in blazes is it?"

"A force beyond your comprehension," Mullane said brusquely. "You were unconscious for two days. It was not used at full power. I hope you won't make that unpleasantness necessary."

"I don't get this, Mully. Where could the rocket go and return the next night? On a trial orbit, maybe? Was it manned?"

He sensed that Mullane, or the likeness of Mullane, had been disturbed about something and was desperately anxious to mollify Temple as far as possible. His willingness to linger and answer questions added to that feeling.

"The rocket," Mullane said quietly, "was flown to the moon by Dr. Rocossen. It carried a prefabricated, air-tight landing depot and portable equipment for launching the return journey. In a few days we shall be ready to begin operations on regular schedule."

"Now, Mully," Temple said with ominous softness, "you are treating me like a mental delinquent. I don't have to be a walking IBM machine to compute distances, speeds and time. No propulsion system on Earth could send a rocket to the moon and back within twenty-four hours."

"My boy," Mullane said, almost jovially, "The system we employ was not created on Earth."

For moments Temple was too staggered to speak. Then he cried, "But why the moon? What's so important on the moon?"

"The only burying ground where the insulation of intervening space will prevent the bodies of Crimson Plague victims from contaminating all humanity. There appears to be no place on or in the Earth where they cannot continue to spread infection. The only salvation of humanity is to remove them from the Earth at once. There seems to be no other way to check the spread of the Plague, prevent world-wide chaos and give medical science the time it needs to develop combative measures."

Temple collapsed on the cot, his jaw sagging. "Then this whole crazy business was just to transport Plague victims to the moon."

"Precisely, Curtis. The government is behind us one hundred per cent, knowing the hope of the world lies with us. The present rocket will transport twenty-five bodies at a time. Work has already begun on one capable of carrying hundreds. An army of workmen is already constructing a landing field outside where special planes can deliver bodies from anywhere on Earth."

"But what protects you and the people who deliver the bodies from contagion? If you know an immunizing agent, for God's sake, give it to the public and stop this slaughter and panic. What is the Crimson Plague anyhow?"

"The meteorites brought the Plague from outer space. We *do* have an immunizing agent, but it will take months to produce it in quantity and in the meantime humanity may be destroyed. This is our only hope of buying time to build defenses. Now I hope you understand, Curtis."

"I think I do," Temple said softly. "The Culwain Expedition

cracked open a meteorite, found the Plague, alerted the government and designed this impossible space travel method to save humanity. Is that about it, Mully?"

"Precisely, Curtis. You are, as I have always said, an extremely perceptive young man."

"And you, Mully," Temple said, "are an unholy damned liar!"

For an instant Mullane's face was almost human in its icy rage. "You—you stupid fool!"

"You're the fool," Temple said wearily, "standing there and trying to tell me these lies. What do you take me for? You geniuses—none of whom has had medical training—expect me to believe you saw organisms the best medical instruments on Earth can't find? And instantly pounced on an immunizing agent for which real doctors have given their lives? Go peddle that to the kiddies on the bedtime story hour, Mully. I'm a big boy, now."

Mullane was already swinging the panel shut. Before it completely closed he snarled, "Our first decision concerning you was clearly a mistake, Curtis. However, a more intense application of the blue beam will correct the error and eliminate further interference."

Through the narrow slit, Temple looked straight into Mullane's eye and delivered his parting shot. "Why bother with something you might have to explain later, Mully? Why don't you just give me the Crimson Plague like the others and cart me off to the moon?"

The panel slammed and the bolt ground home. But in the last fleeting instant Temple was sure that Mullane's face registered a staggering shock.

He listened to the angry beat of Mullane's feet down the corridor outside and his eyes flamed in the granite mask of his face. He wanted to sit and think over Mullane's fantastic story, to sort out the grains of truth he knew were scattered through. But the thinking time was past. In his desperate effort to extract information by needling Mullane, he had obviously skirted dangerously close to some truths.

They could no longer afford to let him live. Temple had no doubt at all his death warrant was already signed and sealed. In a matter of minutes Mullane or an appointed executioner would be back with a weapon and his last chance to save Lee and the rest from their sinister bondage would be ended.

The thought of Lee Mason, doomed to live out her life as the helpless puppet of some inhuman control aroused him to desperation. His mind raced as he searched the barren room for a defense.

He might wrench a club of some kind from the iron cot, but whoever came would be too clever to get within reach. A stab of blue ray through the panel would put him out instantly. Perhaps it could even

52

find him through the wall or closed door, since it had struck through clothing without apparent hindrance.

His frantic gaze fell on the blankets folded across the cot. With desperate haste he ripped the stoutest into long strips, using a sharp edge of the cot frame as a knife. Knotting these together, he fashioned a crude noose, but when he let go the soft loop collapsed. Still, there was nothing else to do but try.

Standing on the cot he worked his noose up through the mesh ceiling over the door, pushed it along past the partition and felt it drop through on the outside. He played out line, hoping no one was in the corridor to notice the dangling loop. He could only guess—and fervently hope—that it hung above the door, high enough to escape notice.

It was such a slender gamble, with so much riding on its success. His palms were wet and he could feel cold sweat gluing his shirt to his back. He fought to keep his hands steady and his nerves keen.

Somewhere a door slammed and hurrying steps pounded close. They sounded like Mullane's swift tread. His heart sank as the steps halted outside the door but were not followed by the grating of the bolt being slid back. If the panel was not opened, and his executioner merely shot a sweeping beam through the door, he was doomed.

"Mully," he called. "Is that you out there? I wanted to tell you that I've been thinking over what you told me and maybe it is the truth. I'd hate to be on the wrong side if your outfit really can save the human race from extinction."

Hardly daring to breathe, he waited until the bolt slid back and the panel opened. "Now it is you who are treating me like a gullible child, Curtis. You're merely stalling, hoping somehow to persuade me to spare your valueless life. It is too late for that."

He lifted the blue beam projector, frowning as he made some adjustment of a stud on the base of the stubby, flaring barrel. Temple's right hand, outside Mullane's line of vision, lifted. The noose on the other end slid down into sight, just over the astronomer's head but too far forward.

Mullane finished his adjustment and leveled the projector. Temple put on an expression of anguished terror and weaved to the side. Mullane had to bend almost to the open panel to see him.

"Don't make this difficult, Curtis. There is no possible escape, as you must know."

Temple's hand snapped upward. The noose dropped squarely onto Mullane's head, started to slip off sideways as he jerked his face upward, then opened and slid down over his ears.

Mullane yelled, Temple dived aside, hauling with all his strength on the makeshift hangman's noose and a lance of bluish light flashed past his face by inches. Then the beam vanished and he heard the clatter of the projector on the corridor floor.

The astronomer was on tiptoe, his face turning dark with suffused blood, small hands clawing futilely at the strangling loop. Temple gritted his teeth and hung on until the hands fell limply away and the face turned purple.

Keeping his line taut, he stretched through the panel, drew Mullane's slight body closer and felt the pockets. There was one key by itself. Stretching his arm to full length, Temple worked it into the lock and suddenly his prison door swung open.

He lowered the limp figure to the floor, tore away the noose and gusted a great sigh of relief when he felt a thread of pulse. Dragging Mullane into the cell room he locked the door and put the key in his own pocket. "Some day you'll thank me for this, Mully," he murmured. "If I'm still alive."

He examined the fallen projector with interest. There were two studs, one apparently controlling intensity, the other inside the curve of butt serving as a trigger. He turned the control stud halfway back and hoped that if he had to use it, it was not set at lethal power.

Escape had no part in his thoughts. He had penetrated the camp but not its deeper mysteries. Until Lee Mason and the rest were freed from their weird captivity he would not leave the camp under his own power. But right now he must find a hiding place until nightfall when he had some chance of moving around with a degree of freedom.

He looked around the great, shadowy cylinder of the tower. A row of small rooms, similar to his late prison, seemed to encircle the base. Outside these was a narrow corridor, formed by a metal wall that encircled the lower part of the crouching rocket. He guessed this was a sort of splash-guard to confine the rocket blast, but it seemed much too low and frail to offer much protection.

But there was no time to study the assembly. Reluctantly he tore himself from contemplation of the towering rocket and looked around for safe cover. Moving warily around the curving corridor he came upon a closed door in the outer wall. Holding his breath he eased it open a crack and peered out. The sight that met his gaze made him stiffen.

He was looking down a wide camp street, thick with lengthening shadows of evening. Pounding toward him through those shadows like a wolf pack in full cry came the entire Meteoritics Team, running in a grim bunch. Rocossen and Jacobs were carrying shotguns. Out in front and leading them was Lee Mason, her lovely face set in cold fury, her slender hands clutching one of blue beam projectors.

They were heading with ominous purposefulness straight toward

54

the door where Temple stood. From their grim manner there was no shadow of doubt in his mind that somehow they knew of his escape and were racing to corner him for the kill.

He lifted his own projector to the crack. One sweep of the paralyzing ray would send them all tumbling. But as his finger tightened on the firing stud the realization came to him that he had no sure knowledge of the setting. For all he knew, it might be powerful enough to deliver serious injury or even death.

He let the projector drop to his side, whirled away and ran. Around a curve in the corridor he saw another outside door and plunged through it, hearing the pounding feet of his hunters enter the corridor.

Temple found himself in a long hall with a closed door at the far end, apparently leading outside. On each side of the hall were small laboratories, each fitted out for research in a different field. He ran past them, toward the far door that offered a hope of breaking out into the dusk where there was more room to flee and more places to hide.

He was almost to his goal when he heard the scrape of feet beyond the door and the knob turned. Someone was coming in. He flung himself through the nearest door and saw, by the special instruments and the racks of lenses and prisms, that this must be the laboratory of Lansdon, the physicist whose special field was optics.

On a small stand stood an instrument so oddly out of place that it caught his attention. At first he thought it was an old-fashioned stereoscope. It had the same kind of hooded viewer with twin square lenses, but instead of the old double cards that produced a three-dimensional picture, the sliding rack held a thin sheet of some richly violet metal that he guessed might be cesium.

For an instant his scientific curiosity made him pause for a closer look. Then the sound of feet in the hall and the closing of the door reminded him of his perilous position.

There were no windows in the lab and only the one door he had just entered. The only possible hiding place was in the deep shadows under the lab bench. He dived for it, hunching as far back as possible as he heard the heavy feet tramp into the room.

Hardly daring to breathe he heard the feet approach. Then he could see a man's legs from the knees down. They moved toward the bench and stopped. There was an ominous silence, and then the familiar voice of Lansdon spoke.

"I am quite aware that you are hiding under my bench, Curtis. Come out quietly. I have a pistol trained on you and I will not hesitate to shoot if necessary."

Temple's breath gusted out. He lifted the projector, hesitated, then tucked it out of sight under his coat and crawled out. He climbed to his feet with weary resignation.

The movement brought his eyes momentarily in line with the screen of the curious instrument on the stand so that he was seeing Lansdon's head and shoulders through the violet film. The sight froze him in gaping amazement.

The image on the screen showed something alien and incredible— a ball of glowing violent luminescence clinging tightly to the nape of Lansdon's neck at the base of his brain. It was like nothing Temple had ever seen before, a globule of pure radiance without form or features. When he looked past the screen, the thing was invisible. Viewed through the film again it was still there, pulsing with a malevolent life of its own.

The mind-shattering discovery had taken only a moment, his own reaction masked too quickly to be noticed. He finished climbing to his feet and met the physicist's furious eyes.

"You have seen too much," Lansdon whispered. He pointed a revolver point-blank and fired.

The tightening of Lansdon's muscles and the rise of the revolver's double action hammer telegraphed the shot, sent Temple plunging aside as the explosion thundered. Liquid fire seared a path along his ribs under his left arm, drove the breath from his lungs with a gasping yelp.

He stumbled, went to his knees and felt breath and strength surge back to his body under the lash of terrible desperation. A table of instruments shielded him briefly. Yelling, Lansdon was starting around the end to get another clear shot. Temple got his hands under the edge of the table and heaved. It went over with a crash of shattering glass, knocking the physicist back against a row of metal supply cabinets, momentarily pinning him.

Before he could jerk his gun hand free, Temple was past and into the hall. He bounced off the opposite wall, snatched the door open and raced out into the night as the whole pack, still led by Lee Mason, burst into the hall from the tower.

Head down, sobbing for breath, Temple pounded down the wide street toward the outside gate. Behind him there were no loud cries or bawling of directions. There was something inexpressibly chilling in that silence, a grim reminder that the *things* had a means of silent communication all their own.

A guard stood in front of the locked gate, cradling a shotgun. Temple could knock him down with the blue ray, throw the automatic gate control switch and escape. But escape was no part of his intention. He swerved, raced between two buildings and doubled back toward the tower.

It was a crazy, suicidal action. He was stumbling with exhaustion,

56

his wounded side was a knife of pain, his shirt stiff with blood. But now that he knew so much of the terrible truth, his mind was locked on one desperate purpose.

From the deep shadows, he saw his pursuers separating, fanning out with flashlights whipping back and forth to probe every possible hiding place. He saw Lee Mason, gripping projector and flashlight, swing aside to cover a parallel street. Like a grim ghost, he drifted after her. At every step he expected her invisible control to detect his presence and warn her, as it had apparently done for Spirovic and Lansdon.

Now, for some reason that left him baffled, it had apparently deserted her. She reached the end of the street and stopped, flashing the beam of her light along the fence. Temple's running feet made no sound on the soft dirt. Her first inkling of danger was the encircling arm like a band of steel and the hand that muffled her outcry.

She fought him viciously, with an unexpected strength that took all his effort to counter. He gasped in agony as her elbow slammed his wounded side, gasped again as sharp heels drummed against his shins. He could feel her teeth snapping savagely in an effort to bite the muffling palm. His right hand caught her flailing wrist and twisted mercilessly until limp fingers let go of the deadly projector.

Temple felt himself weakening. The throbbing wound seemed to be draining his left arm of strength. If the violent jerking of her head freed her mouth for even a moment, her cry would bring help. There had to be an end to the struggle at any cost.

He used his last waning strength to pull her head back and her chin up. His right released her suddenly and came up in a chopping arc. Knuckles slammed into the line of slender jaw with brutal force and her body went limp.

Cold-eyed and grim, Temple hoisted her over his shoulder and squatted down, panting, to feel for the projector and flashlight. He jammed both into his pocket and looked around. His purpose was not yet accomplished while that circle of deadly fence hemmed him within the hostile camp. While the floodlights seemed to be still out of order, a few scattered streetlights were on. He was grimly sure that their first move had been to restore current to the fence.

His gaze fell on the row of parked trucks. He stumbled to the nearest and found the ignition key in the lock. He hoisted Lee's limp body into the cab, climbed under the wheel and toed the starter. The engine roared to life, alerting the scattered searchers to his whereabouts and intent. Temple clashed the gears and sent the heavy vehicle around and out onto the main street that led to the gate.

He glimpsed darting flash beams and wondered vaguely why no deadly blue ray reached out for him. Then the truck was thundering toward the brightly lighted gate.

The guard was in the road, leveling a pistol. Temple saw the wink of scarlet flame and heard the impact of slugs against the truck body. A corner of the windshield sprouted a pattern of diverging lines and broken glass showered over Lee's huddled form.

Cold-eyed and grim, Temple got out one of the projectors, leaned from the cab window and pressed the stud. The blue ray lanced out and the guard collapsed like a punctured balloon. The truck skidded around him to a halt. Temple leaped down, ran to the shack and threw a switch just inside the door. Motors hummed and the gate began to swing open.

He whirled back, bent over the guard and gusted a breath of relief when he felt a steady pulse. Then the projector was set to stun, not kill, and he could use it with impunity. He ran back to the truck and sent it roaring out through the gate to freedom.

At the juncture of the dirt road with the main highway he stopped the truck and looked back. There were no signs of pursuit. He rummaged through the cab and found a coil of light rope that was probably used to secure small loads. With this he tied Lee's wrists and ankles. He knew the bonds were cruelly tight, but he also knew the savage cunning of the power that possessed her and far more than comfort was involved.

He let the motor idle and sat gripping the wheel, trying to plot his next move. He had Lee safe for the moment from the physical clutches of the group and he had at least a vague idea now of what was behind the sickening personality change. But he had no idea at all of how to bring her back to normal, or even if such a thing were possible.

He knew only that he had to find a haven somewhere with the equipment to work and search for the hidden answer. All usual laboratories would be closed to him now. In the eyes of the law he was a car thief, a kidnaper and probably worse, and he had no doubt at all that the group in the camp would press every possible charge to hamper him.

Mullane's claim to government support was no exaggeration. The whole power of the nation would be arrayed against him to "rescue" Lee and punish him. If he tried to tell the incredible truth as far as he knew it, he would undoubtedly be rushed to the nearest mental hospital and committed for life.

Suddenly the thought of the one possible haven, the one person he knew who would believe him and help him, no matter what the risk. Allen Farge, who had been his roommate and closest friend through college, was now head of the Physics Department at Rocky Mountain Tech. If anyone could help him now, it would be Farge. It was a gamble, but now every breath was a gamble.

Beside him Lee stirred and whimpered. He bent over her, his fingers probing the soft golden cloud of her hair. It might have been overwrought imagination but he was sure his fingertips felt a faint electric tingling at the back of her head. There was no doubt in his mind that whether he actually felt it or not, the sinister thing was still there.

She opened her eyes, glared around wildly, then spat at him with an animal snarl of rage. "You fool! What have you done? Untie me and take me back to the camp immediately."

"Take it easy," Temple said quietly. "I know what I'm facing now and I've tied those ropes to stay tied. There'll be no freedom until I've found out exactly what you are and how you can be destroyed. You know I'm not speaking to Lee Mason now. I am speaking to *you*—the thing that has attached itself to her head and taken over her mind and will. I know you're there. I saw you, or a piece of you, on Lansdon's head when I accidentally looked through the detector device he had. I don't know what you are, except that you're a shining blob of something evil that has turned Lee and Lansdon and all those others into mindless robots. I don't know now, but I'll find out."

"You're insane!" Lee panted. "What kind of mad talk is that? Don't you realize that what you're doing is kidnapping me? And in case you have forgotten, the penalty for kidnapping is the electric chair."

"I haven't forgotten," Temple said, his eyes terrible in their cold determination. "And you might remember that since I have already earned that ultimate penalty, I couldn't suffer anything worse for murder. Lee Mason means more to me than my life. If at any time I see that I am going to be captured or otherwise prevented from finishing what I've started, I will destroy this lovely shell of her before I'll see it go on to a lifetime of slavery. Think *that* over before you force her to scream for help while we're in a gas station or passing through towns."

He put the truck into gear and rolled onto the highway, turning away from Bomer, heading west toward Denver.

CHAPTER 10

Battle Is Joined

It was four o'clock in the morning, a day later, when he swung the truck into the driveway of a pleasant home on a tree-lined Denver street. His throat tightened as he remembered how often he had been a guest in this house, enjoying the warm hospitality, the all-night talks with Allen Farge when their kindred imaginations roamed to the farthest reaches of the universe.

He looked at Lee, huddled silently in the corner of the seat. "I'm leaving you for a few minutes. You're plotting ways to defeat and destroy me, of course, and you may succeed because you seem to possess the devil's own science. But here's something to bear in mind. You can't control me as you do these others. You tried that night through Mullane and the Solles, and you've undoubtedly tried since when I was inside the camp and menacing your whole scheme. Furthermore, I think I know why you can't and if my guess is right, that's a weakness I can use to defeat you."

The fleeting blaze of fury in Lee's eyes told him that his shot had struck home. She glared at him in silent hatred. He put the ignition key in his pocket and opened the cab door.

"You know I'm a deadly menace to you, but you can't read my mind to discover what I'm up to. Your only hope of smashing me is to control someone close to me. No one will ever be closer than Lee Mason. If you ever get the idea of destroying her and taking over someone else, you'd better think twice. Alive, she is your only hope of keeping watch on me and stopping me."

Walking toward the house, he found himself trembling and perspiring from the strain. He *thought* he had planted a safeguard against any harm to Lee, but he could never really be sure.

Listening to the endless melody of the door chimes, Temple began to feel a sick fear that Farge might have gone away on a summer vacation. Then suddenly an ornamental lantern over his head flashed on. The square-jawed, homely face of Allen Farge peered sleepily out through the door pane. Then the sleepy look whipped away and the door was jerked open.

"Holy boiled owls in a bread basket! *Curt*, you rumpled Romeo, get the blazes in here. What are you doing out in this neck of the woods besides gladdening my heart?" He squinted and made a face. "Eegads!

60

You look like a bad accident on its way to happen. Boy, you need a good stiff drink."

Temple grinned in weary relief. "You, my good man, are *so* right. And fix yourself one just as stiff. You're going to need it when you hear my story."

Farge grabbed his arm. "Straight ahead to the kitchen. If you say the word, I'll mix up a washtub full."

They compromised on tall glasses, bickering amiably over measurements and mixers. But when they had seated themselves at the kitchen table, the light laughter went out of Farge's face.

"All right, Curt," he said quietly. "Down a couple of good slugs and get on with it. You're not here on any jolly social visit. That look in the back of your eyes would scare a witch off her broomstick. Let's have it."

Temple told him everything from the mystery of the stony meteorites bombarding Kansas to the harrowing flight from the camp. At mention of the Crimson Plague, Farge's lips tightened.

"I've seen victims of the Plague and I don't want to see any more. Do you really think those *things* are behind it?"

Temple nodded. "I'm almost sure of it, Al. And I'm just as sure that the reason bacteriologists can't find Plague germs is because there aren't any germs. Maybe the cause is a filterable virus too small for even the electron microscope to pick up. Or it may be caused by something completely foreign to any knowledge we possess. But I just can't swallow their offer to transport Plague victims to the moon as altogether an altruistic gift to humanity. I haven't seen a speck of evidence that they give one damn about humanity. I don't know what the purpose of their fantastic setup is, but I'm betting it's just plain evil."

"You," Farge said, "have the kind of nasty, suspicious mind I admire. I'm crazy enough to keep listening as long as you go on making two and two add up to four." Temple described the effect of the blue beam and passed over one of the projectors for his friend to examine. Farge's eyes gleamed with interest. "Count me in on whatever you decide to do, Curt. All I ask is a chance to take this gadget apart and try to find out what makes it tick."

Temple nodded. "It's a promise. Is your school out for the summer, Al? I've lost track of time these past weeks."

"It closed last week, my family's on a long trip, and twenty miles up in the mountains I've got one of the neatest little private laboratories you ever laid eyes on. I built it for a spot to hide out in and fool around with off-beat experiments. It's at your disposal, along with any help I can give. But what's on your mind, Curt? What line of attack can you possibly launch against an unseeable, untouchable menace such as you describe?"

"There's only one I can think of. Somehow I've got to duplicate that detector I saw in Lansdon's lab, the one that made the entity visible to my eyes. We've got to be able to see them before we can fight them, Al. Until we can make those things visible at will, we can't analyze their nature or perfect any sure weapon. That's item one on the agenda."

Farge whistled. "As a warm-up for that little odd job, we might practice catching sunbeams in a butterfly net."

Temple grinned tiredly. "I've got a few notions shaping up on what that thing was and how to build one like it. But it's too complex to go into right now. I'm too pooped to make sense."

"You should be, after a siege like that," Farge said. "But to copy something that by all the laws of physics can't possibly exist..." He shook his head. "You don't even have one of those entities, as you call them, for a guinea pig to show you when you hit the jackpot."

"Oh, but I do have," Temple said quietly, and for the first time he told of the capture of Lee Mason. He finished, "So you can see what kind of Federal charges you'd be laying yourself in for if you throw in with me on this job."

Farge leaped to his feet so violently that his chair went crashing over. His eyes were wild. "To hell with that! But do you mean to tell me you've left that poor kid tied up out there in the cold all this time? That's inhuman."

"Take it easy, Al. That 'poor kid' would happily slit your throat and mine in a moment if she could get loose. That isn't Lee Mason out there. It's a hellish, inhuman thing that has usurped her body. God only knows whether or not her real personality still exists. Maybe if the thing in her brain were destroyed, she would die—or worse yet, have no mind of her own left. I've tried not to think of those possibilities, because nothing must keep me from finishing what I started, no matter what the cost."

Farge gripped his shoulder for a moment in silent sympathy. "We'll fight it together, Curt. But what's to prevent our being taken over, just as she was, by those things?"

"In your case, nothing. That's why I don't dare let you get near her, at least until I've tried something. They haven't been able to get into my brain, and during the long drive I think I figured out why. If I'm right, I can give you the same protection I have before we go any further." He grinned wryly. "Al, does your willingness to help include sacrificing all the family sterling silver, and do you have a crucible or something I can use to melt it down in a hurry?"

"Yes, to both questions," Farge said promptly. "Let's go." While a mass of sterling tableware and silver dishes melted slowly over a Bunsen burner in the basement, Temple explained his theory. "I'm convinced that it's the silver plate in the back of my head that keeps them from reaching my brain. I can't think of any other reason for my apparent immunity."

"But why silver?" Farge demanded.

Temple shrugged tiredly. "Don't ask me—except that silver is opaque to ultraviolet radiations beyond thirty-three hundred angstrom units, and the thing I saw had a sort of violet color. Maybe it's a form of congealed radiation in that range. Anyhow, all we can do is give it a try."

"But if those things are so smart, why haven't they figured it out and done something about it in your case, Curt?"

"I'm sure they know, all right. But during the two days I was a prisoner, they were occupied in getting their rocket into operation. Besides, there's no surgeon in the group and removing my screen would be a delicate operation at best."

"Then why not just knock you off and be done with it?"

"I don't want to sound too modest, my boy, but it's barely possible they think my feeble brain contains some scraps of information that are important to their plans."

The sun was above the horizon when Temple led Farge, looking grotesque in a thin skull cap of hammered silver, out to the truck where Lee huddled, wide awake and glaring. For a long moment she and Farge stared at one another with a strange intensity while Temple watched, almost afraid to breathe. At last Lee flung herself back in the seat, panting.

"It couldn't get through, Curt," Farge said quietly. "I think you've won this round."

They rode up to the mountain laboratory in the truck, with Lee slumped dully between them. It seemed a safer hiding place for the Culwain truck in case an alarm had been spread. Although he desperately needed sleep, the small triumph had filled him with a new energy and determination. If the luminous menaces could be defeated on one front, there was renewed hope of victory in larger battles.

* * * *

An hour later, Temple stared with admiration across one of the most complete private labs he had ever seen. It occupied half of a comfortable log lodge nestled among pines on the mountainside at the end of a private lane. Luxurious living quarters included a spare bedroom, but Temple grimly vetoed using it as a prison for Lee.

"The window's too convenient, the door too frail, and there isn't an adequate lock."

They settled finally on a stout, windowless storeroom off the laboratory and fitted it up as a comfortable but reasonably escape-proof cell. A bank of steel shelving on one wall bothered Farge. "She could rip those down and make a dangerous club out of one of those metal uprights, Curt."

"We'll risk it," Temple decided. "I'm gambling that we've scared the thing a little by learning a couple of its secrets. I think it will stay quietly, using her to keep an eye on us until it discovers what our danger quotient really is. The thing I'm most of afraid of is having it abandon her now, maybe even destroy her in retaliation, and turn to some new angle of attack we can't anticipate or guard against. I've tried to throw enough scare into it to block such a move, but against the power it seems to have, my efforts seem pitifully puny."

He paced the laboratory, driving a clenched fist into his palm. "Damn it, Al, everything we have is guesswork. It scares the pants off me. How do I know I'm right about any of it? I *thought* I saw a ball of light on a man's head, and out of that I've built up a theory that might be completely cockeyed."

"What are those things and what are their powers? Sometimes they seem superintelligent and at other times they seem to be dreaming. I've pieced odds and ends of clues into a crazy picture that might be all wrong. How do we know it isn't a picture deliberately planted to throw us off the track?"

"You saw the thing," Farge pointed out quietly, "and you were on the track with your silver-cap theory."

Temple clutched his head and groaned. "Sure. But for all we know, the place is swarming with the things right now, holding a council of war over the best means to smash us. It's all such blind shots in the dark."

"We've shot in the dark all our lives, Curt. We were using workable blueprints of atomic structure before anyone had ever seen an atom. We've located, weighed, measured and analyzed dark stars we still can't see. It's essentially the same sort of job."

"Don't mind me," Temple grinned wryly. "There's nothing actually wrong that a little sleep can't cure."

"Before you cork off, I'm puzzled about something. You said there were over a thousand workmen in that camp and suppliers outside who had their minds monkeyed with so they couldn't spill important beans. Does that mean there are enough of those blasted entity things so everybody had one riding him?"

Temple spread his hands helplessly. "Could be, though somehow I

64

doubt it. My guess is that they only enter those minds long enough to alter the memory pattern, like changing a printed radio circuit. I think they can either simply erase a portion or plant a prearranged pattern that will keep their dupes doing only what they've been ordered to without supervision. It may be a little like planting a post-hypnotic suggestion. The ones they stay with are those like Lee and the team, whose minds and skills they need constantly."

Farge was staring out the window over vistas of mountains clothed in pine and aspen. Without turning he said softly, "Curt, do you suppose while those things were inside someone's skull they could tamper with the autonomous nervous system, like making that person's blood all rush to his head and face, making him fall into a state of catalepsy or suspended animation that can be mistaken for death?"

Temple stared at him, his eyes bloodshot, his face haggard and gray with fatigue. He whispered, "The Crimson Plague..."

CHAPTER 11

Counterattack

The new concept of the Plague added barbs to the lash of desperation that drove them. They became more robot than human themselves, with every nerve in their bodies crying: *Faster! Faster!*

The mountains blocked television but Farge's radio kept them informed of events outside. Apparently the entities had met the challenge by redoubling their own hellish activities.

The Crimson Plague was spreading with increased speed, leaping oceans to ravage Europe, Asia and Africa and strike ships at sea. Australia cowered, waiting for the first blow to come. Major cities were emptying as panic-stricken people fled with no place to go.

The moon flights bearing Plague victims had become daily affairs and the new enlarged rocket was almost ready for service. The parade of planes carrying victims from all over the Earth to the field beside the camp had grown so heavy that a traffic control system had to be installed and manned around the clock.

A Bomer woman was committed to a mental hospital for insisting she had seen her husband working at the camp after he had been supposedly shipped to the moon as a Plague corpse. Temple and Farge exchanged wordless looks and stepped up their efforts another impossible notch.

Temple had drawn a rough sketch of Lansdon's detector as detailed as he could remember and this was their blueprint for the search.

"It's a stereoscope," he told Farge, "designed to superimpose the image of the invisible object over the visual image in correct physical relationship. One of the two viewing lenses was, as I told you, opaque, the other apparently an ordinary ground glass magnifier. The black lens could have been ground from Wood's nickel oxide glass. We know that Wood's glass filters out visible light rays but permits the passage of ultraviolet light. I'd almost bet that's the answer to the lens assembly, so there'd be no problem there. Our real headache will lie in that film of violet-colored metal where I saw the combined image."

Farge nodded and chewed his lip. "Well, films made from the alkali metals will pass short-wave light below the visible spectrum. But you said that particular film had a definite violet shade, which lets out lithium, sodium, potassium and rubidium. They block all visible light and therefore show only dead black. Cesium, the heaviest of that group, allows some of the visible violet to get through so it would have a violet tint. Your suggestion of trying cesium seems logical, but it almost seems too easy, Curt."

"It probably is," Temple admitted, "but it's at least some kind of starting point to work from. We might as well try all the alkali metals with every known type of fluorescent screen and see how far we get."

Farge nodded eagerly. "Just give me something besides all Xs to put in a formula and I can try working it out mathematically. While we're waiting for a Wood's lens and the stock of alkali metal films to come, what do you say we test that thing on Lee's head for ultraviolet radiations? We can see if it fogs a photographic plate, emits measurable electrons or reacts on a fluorescent pigment by direct bombardment."

They plunged into the new tests with boundless enthusiasm. Farge remained optimistic even after repeated failures as one experiment suggested another or opened a whole new path to be explored. In sharp contrast, Temple's early hopes dwindled rapidly to a dark depression of spirit.

"It's Lee," he explained glumly when Farge questioned him worriedly. "Haven't you noticed how meek and cooperative she's gotten since we started these tests? Even when she remembers to fight and snarl at us, it's plainly just acting. Most of the time she sits there, looking like the cat that ate the canary and trying not to laugh in our fat, foolish faces while we play our silly games with the back of her head."

"Come to think of it," Farge said, startled, "I believe you're right, Curt. Does that mean…?"

"It means," Temple said harshly, "that we're so far off the right track that we aren't even worth glaring at any more."

Farge pounded a determined fist on the bench. "One of these fine days we'll change that smile, Curt. You just wait and see."

They cut sleep to three hours out of the twenty-four and ate only when weakness reminded them of the need for fuel on the fires of their driving energy. Both looked ten years older.

At the end of a week they faced the grim truth.

"We've flopped," Farge said bitterly. "A week of trying everything we can think of without an inch of progress to show for it. We can't even be sure that thing's still on her head any more. We can't see it or feel it or get a flicker of response on any energy detecting device known. For all we know, the thing could have set up a mental pattern telling her how to act for the next ten years and then gone off to find a new body to haunt."

He was talking across the top of Lee Mason's bent head. She sat between them on the stool she occupied for their tests, her eyes demurely downcast. In the week of endless tests they had both forgotten her presence most of the time, except as another piece of inanimate laboratory equipment.

Her own meekness and silence made the illusion easy to accept.

Temple shrugged discouragedly and stared at the floor. His gaunt body slumped with weariness and strain. Suddenly he tensed, threw back his shoulders and looked at Farge with blazing eyes.

"Wait a minute! I started by describing that thing wholly in terms of physical light and energy, and we've been sticking to that one track in our search ever since."

"What else could it be?" Farge asked dully.

"Mental energy," Temple cried. "Biophysics has proven that thoughts are electrical, or at least that they produce definite measurable electrical currents. Now, this entity apparently merges itself with brain activity, so why couldn't it be pure brain energy, or something closely related?"

Farge looked startled. "But biophysics can detect mental and nerve currents, even measure them and time the speed of their flow. We've used most of the same instruments here without getting any response of any kind. Besides, mind energy doesn't fall in the ultraviolet band, Curt, but it was a good theory."

"It still is," Temple said, "a sound one. Look, a generator *produces* electric current but it isn't electricity in itself. Think of this entity as a generator instead of its product. We're not positive about the nature of mind energy yet. Suppose it really belongs in a whole undiscovered spectrum of energies that may coexist with our familiar spectrum but only touch or impinge on it in one spot—such as the ultraviolet band. That might seem fantastic but instead of hunting for facts to fit theories, let's examine some theories that fit facts."

"Sure," Farge said, looking bewildered, "but how are you going to prove it with existing instruments, or make any use of the knowledge if you did prove it?"

Temple had been staring intently at the polished brass base of a desk lamp. He whirled, his face alight with new hope. "Get her locked up and get back here fast, Al. We're on our way."

Farge raced back in a moment, his face eager. "You've hit on something, Curt. Tell me quick."

"I hit the answer," Temple said gleefully, "and proved it. I happened to be watching Lee's reflection in that lamp base as I was rambling along on the mind-energy and unknown-spectrum idea. If looks could kill, I'd be dead right now. The expression on her face for an unguarded instant was the best evidence in the world that I'd stumbled on to the main track to our answer."

"But my Lord, Curt," Farge said, mopping his face, "you're

blithely talking about moving into a wholly unknown science. We don't know its simplest fundamentals. We haven't any tools or instruments—"

"Then we'll create them," Temple interrupted. "You took that blue beam projector apart and couldn't find a battery or any recognizable power source, and it's been driving you nuts. What you found was a gold grid in a sliding frame in front of a slice of unfamiliar and unidentifiable crystal. Give your thinking a twist and tackle it again, Al."

"All my thinking seems to be twisted," Farge said irritably. "I don't get you at all."

"That gadget doesn't generate energy at all, man. It only concentrates natural energy the way a burning glass concentrates sunlight. Find that natural energy and we've got it." He paced the floor, his tired face lighted by the glow of fresh excitement, his weary brain spurred to a new burst of life. He snapped his fingers. "There's one screen we've never tried—element 87, moldavium. It's one of the alkali metals but little is known about its properties because it resists efforts to isolate it in pure form. Maybe somewhere it exists in pure form now, or those entities found out how to isolate it. If they did it, we can. Order a supply right away, air express, in its purest available form, and we'll take it from there."

It was late the next afternoon when, in the midst of another experiment, Temple suddenly shouted. "Oh, what a dope I've been! Cosmic rays! That's our whole answer, Al. That's the radiation that destroys the entities. It's been right there in front of me all the time and I couldn't see it."

"I still can't, Curt."

"I told you about stony meteorites slamming onto Kansas all these years with a concentration too great to be random. That implies intelligent bombardment for a purpose. Don't ask me why Kansas; I haven't gotten that far. But suppose the entities were responsible, yet as far as we know, none ever tried taking over people before. So we can safely guess that none ever survived the journey before."

Farge's jaw dropped. "You mean all those meteorites that hit Kansas started out with a load of the things?"

"Not all, but enough to upset the law of averages for distribution of natural meteorite falls. But until now, no entity survived the trip because of unshielded cosmic rays in space. According to Stilwell, the FBI man, this last swarm was covered with an unfamiliar pitch coating that might well have been some new kind of shielding. If so, it explains why these entities came through alive to start their deviltry on Earth— and what we must have to destroy them."

"But Curt, cosmic rays average six *billion* volts of energy, more

69

than we could ever generate. And nothing short of a couple of hundred tons of magnets can concentrate them."

"Or," Temple said, "a little slice of alien crystal that might just act on them like a burning glass on sunlight. We've got a Wilson cloud chamber with a Geiger-Müller counter. Let's start shooting the projector into it with that sliding grid at different settings and see what we can photograph in the nature of explosion trails."

As though Temple's idea had supplied a key, the door suddenly swung open for them into a whole new world of discovery. The projector tapped not just one narrow band but a whole unsuspected range of free energy in variable intensities.

Two days later, on a film of semi-refined moldavium, they saw a dull violet glow that moved when Lee Mason's head moved. The image was faint and undefined, and it lacked the stereoscopic image Temple had seen on Lansdon's screen, but it gave them all they needed.

At last they could actually see the presence of entities. And with the ability to see their target, they could at last begin to develop a weapon with which to destroy it.

They were too exhausted to celebrate the first major breakthrough in their struggle. They hung up the negatives of their latest cloud chamber photographs to dry and fell on their beds without stopping to undress.

That night the alarmed enemy struck back.

Temple awoke in inky darkness, bathed in cold perspiration. His lungs heaved in a wracking struggle for air and his nostrils burned with a stinging torment. He lay for a moment, gasping and trying to focus bleary eyes on what seemed to be a parade of gray ghosts that writhed and danced across a patch of moonlight.

Abruptly his brain threw off the bonds of sleep and brought him a horrified realization of what he was seeing. He sprang out of bed, snatched open his door and recoiled from a solid wall of acrid smoke that filled the hall outside.

Fire! The lodge was on fire. He could hear no sound to indicate that either Farge or Lee Mason were alive or conscious.

With a cold terror clawing at his nerves he stumbled to the bathroom, soaked a towel to cover nose and mouth and plunged into the smoke. He fumbled his way down the hall to Farge's bedroom. The air inside was clear, the smoke kept out by a tight-fitting door, and Farge was snoring in blissful ignorance of the peril.

Temple shook him roughly. "Al, wake up! The place is on fire. I don't know how it started or how bad it is, but I've got to get Lee out of that death trap she's locked in. You try to save the most important instruments and those last negatives."

70

He left Farge running for a wet towel to protect his own lungs and plunged out into the wall of smoke. It was thick and acrid but he could hear no crackle of flames nor see a glow of fire. With fear cold in his heart he felt his way across the smoke-filled laboratory to the door of her prison. He was feeling for the sliding bolt when the door swung open.

The overhead light still worked and by its pale glow he read the story. The storage cabinet lay on the floor showing a glint of raw metal where the thin sheet-steel leg had been patiently bent back and forth until it broke off. With the jagged edge as a chisel she had gouged a hole in the door big enough for her slender hand to reach the bolt.

He stared dully at the empty room, coughing. The thing that controlled Lee had been panicked into this. It had driven her to break out, set the building on fire and flee.

Farge stumbled through the smoke, almost sobbing, carrying a tangle of wreckage in his arms. "Curt...look! The detector we just finished and your projector—smashed to pieces. Those negatives are gone and the phone has been torn from the wall and hammered to bits."

Temple whirled and snatched one of the fire extinguishers from the lab wall. "Come on. The fire must have been started in the basement. Maybe we can get it under control."

A pile of broken boxes had been heaped under the wooden stairway, paper and shavings dumped on top and the fire started in twists of paper underneath. It was still smoldering but in a moment it would reach the shavings and explode into a roaring inferno.

Temple kicked the boxes away, then thrust the extinguisher into Fargo's hands. "Douse it good, Al. It hasn't gotten a start yet, which means Lee can't have gotten far since setting it. I'm going after her."

He had reached the top of the stairs when he heard the wail of a starter and then the explosive bark of firing cylinders. The sound came from close by. Temple yelled, "Al, she's getting away in the truck!" and sprinted for the door.

He plunged through the dense smoke, slammed into an invisible bench and staggered on to the door. The truck was completing a tight turn toward the narrow road. In the dim dawn light he could see Lee at the wheel, struggling to shift cold-stiffened gears. He sprinted and was almost to the cab when the gears meshed with a grinding crash and the truck lunged ahead.

Temple made a leaping dive and his hands caught the edge of the window frame. He hung on, taking enormous lunging steps to keep his balance as she speeded up, looking frantically for a place to swing up and brace his feet until he could get the cab door open.

He was still trying when Lee leaned out and slammed an iron jack

71

handle across the side of his face. Lights exploded in his eyes, his feet tangled and his grip on the cab door broke. He fell and rolled endlessly into darkness.

Temple awoke with Farge patting cold water on his face and neck. Aside from skinned flesh, a stiff neck and a throbbing bruise along his jawline he seemed to be in fair shape. He sat up groggily.

"There was no use trying to chase her on foot," Farge said, "so I didn't try."

Temple put his face in his hands and groaned. "It's losing her right now that hurts, Al—just when we were on the verge of freeing her from that hellish influence. At any moment now we would have found the weapon to destroy it."

"We already had," Farge said grimly. "I found the last cloud chamber negatives down where she'd tucked them among the shavings to be burned up in her fire. We can't be sure without Johnson asymmetry measurements, of course, but a couple of those vapor trails look to me as if we'd been shooting in something with an energy value of well over five billion volts. That's in the range of cosmic rays. It looks as if we've proved you were right, Curt, but too late to do anything about it. She didn't leave us enough of that projector to tell whether it was vegetable or mineral."

Temple scrambled up, his aches forgotten. "Allen, we've got another projector, safe and intact. I snatched it that same night but I've kept it hidden even from you for fear that entity might peek into your mind somehow and learn about it. All we have to do is duplicate our last setting and go on from there."

"Eeowie!" Farge shouted like a schoolboy. "And we had a scrap of moldavium left over. I tucked it away in the safe. It will be big enough to make up one small detector."

"Then we're in business, boy. Make this one so I can wear it on my forehead like a sun visor. I'll be able to look through it by simply bending my head a little and my hands will be free to work the projector."

Farge stopped short. "Now, just a minute. If you have the idea you can buck that crowd alone, even with the projector, you'd better forget it. You told me yourself they've got the blue paralyzing beam, an army of goons and plenty of conventional weapons. They also have a supreme contempt for any human life that tries to stand in their way. You can't hope to face them alone."

"I've got news for you," Temple said soberly. "You and I *are* alone—alone against practically the whole world. Haven't you been listening to the radio? Where their planes airlift the bodies of Plague victims for transportation to the moon, the epidemic has practically died out. Everywhere else it's spreading like wildfire. Is it any wonder most of the world's convinced humanity's survival depends on that unselfish little group in Kansas? How far do you think we'd get with our crazy theories against that kind of evidence? Just about as far as the nearest booby hatch."

"But if we could get to a few top men, Curt, show them what we've discovered, persuade them to use their influence—"

"While the entities sit back and let them use it?"

Farge's face set in dogged lines. "They can be blocked by a silver shield."

"Oh, sure," Temple said bitterly. "I can just picture us ringing the White House doorbell and saying, 'Mr. President, there are millions of invisible blobs floating around, lousing up people's brains. The only salvation is for you and everyone else to wear one of these clumsy, uncomfortable, expensive and silly-looking skullcaps night and day.' We'd be in strait jackets in no time."

For a minute there was silence. Then Farge's shoulders lifted in a heavy sigh. "Oh, hell, let's get back to work, Curt. At least, I'm on your side for keeps."

"I'd rather have you than the Pentagon," Temple said. With the windows open and a fresh breeze clearing out the smoke, they settled down to their interrupted work. Despite their good luck in having saved a projector and sufficient moldavium, a mood of gloom had settled over their spirits and would not be lifted.

Temple could not forget that he had lost his chance to save Lee by a matter of hours. His somber gaze went to the bench by the wrecked door where a replica of Farge's silver cap lay. He had hammered it out the first day in the lab and kept it there, awaiting their moment of triumph. If somehow they succeeded in destroying or driving out the entity that enslaved her, the cap would be her guarantee of continued freedom. He wondered now if there would ever be an opportunity to use it.

Farge had been occupied with his own dark thoughts, his face haggard, his eyes haunted. He looked up suddenly. "Curt, I keep thinking of what you said about the Crimson Plague being deliberately caused by those things for some purpose of their own. If you're right, and all those victims have only been in a state of suspended animation, what about the hundreds or thousands who've been buried or cremated or dumped into the sea in the wild panic to halt its spread?"

"They were murdered," Temple said harshly. "Cruelly and callously murdered by people who couldn't know any better. I can't forget Stilwell, the first victim, burned up in that shed while I stood by with the mob and let it happen. It's one of the scores I mean to settle with those things…if I live long enough."

Night had closed down before their tasks were completed. A new detector, slightly smaller than the original, was finished. With Lee gone, there was no entity to test it on but every detail of the original had been faithfully duplicated and there was no reason to think this would not work as well. Temple had fashioned a light harness that fitted snugly to his head and held the detector snugly against his forehead. By tilting his head forward slightly he could bring the lenses to eye level. He tried it, bringing the moldavium screen to bear on every part of the roomy laboratory.

"Either we goofed," he said, more cheerfully, "or there are no entities prowling here. I'm inclined to think if there were any here, we'd see them with this."

"And shoot 'em down with this," Farge said, matching Temple's lightened mood as he held up the projector. "I've been checking the new cloud chamber shots and apparently we've got the same setting we used last night. The vapor trails show this thing is delivering either cosmic rays or something with an equal energy range. I almost wish a couple of those invisible glowworms would come around so we could try it out."

"You may get your wish, Al. By now Lee may be back at the camp reporting everything we've been doing and exactly how far along we've gotten. It's a cinch they'll strike back at us in one way or another, and soon. We're too dangerous now to be left alone."

Farge's face clouded. "Curt, I'm bothered about what this projector puts out. We know we're all being bombarded night and day by cosmic rays without harm. They're of such tremendous velocity that they shoot right through our bodies. But we can't be certain that what we have here is the same, or as harmless. For all we know, this might kill anyone it touches. We wouldn't dare turn it on Lee Mason or any of those others until we'd tested it first on some kind of guinea pigs to make sure."

"There will be such a test," Temple said grimly. "It's my theory and my gamble. I want you to turn that projector on me right now and pull the trigger. If I survive, we'll know what we have and what to do with it. If I don't, you'll have to carry on alone, Allen. You know as much about the problem now as I do."

"Curt," Farge protested. "I won't let you take that risk. An energy bombardment of five or ten billion volts could kill you instantly, or destroy brain cells and leave you a mindless imbecile. We can at least test it on laboratory animals first."

"We don't have any animals and we don't have time to order them now. This is coming to a head too fast. At any moment we can expect the counterattack from the entities, and whatever form that takes we can be sure of one thing: It will be nasty."

"All the more reason for you to be alive and fighting back."

74

"There's another consideration," Temple said quietly. "The most important of all, Al. According to the radio, their new moon rocket is completed. Day after tomorrow it is scheduled to blast off for the moon with five hundred Plague victims on board. Five hundred innocent people face some horror we can't even imagine—unless I can stop that flight. If I can take the beam from that projector and survive, I'm leaving at once. Don't forget, I might have to walk clear back to Denver to get a car."

Behind them a quiet voice said, "I wouldn't be in too much of a hurry to leave if I were you."

Temple and Farge spun around, gaping. Just inside the lab door stood two young men with grim faces and sharp, watchful eyes. Each held a stubby pistol centered steadily on them. Beside them stood Lee Mason, an expression of grim triumph on her face.

The taller man held a small, flat folder that was vaguely familiar. He flipped it open. "I'm Tillotson, Federal Bureau of Investigation, and this is my partner, Mr. Rowe. This young lady has preferred charges against you two for kidnapping and unlawful detention. Will you come along quietly, please?"

CHAPTER 12

Flight

Temple stood rigid, the blood draining from his face. Beside him he heard Farge's labored breathing. The two FBI men were looking curiously at the detector jutting from the harness above his eyes. Lee was also eyeing it warily. The projector lay on the bench behind Farge, hidden by his bulky figure.

Tillotson spoke again, his voice sharper. "Well? I have the warrant here if you insist on seeing it. Let's go."

"Wait," Farge said sharply. "This is either the end of everything or a beginning, Curt, and there's only one way to find out. No matter what happens, you're the best qualified to carry on."

Temple shouted, "Allen...*don't*!" But he was too late. Farge snatched up the projector and put the barrel against the side of his head.

Lee Mason screamed. It was a cry of shock and horror, wrung from her by the unexpected sight of an undamaged projector. The FBI men were momentarily paralyzed by the suddenness of Farge's movement, the appearance of something resembling a gun, and most of all by Lee's piercing shriek.

In that instant, when time stood still, Farge pressed the trigger stud. He went rigid, then crumpled to the floor, the projector dropping from his limp hand.

Temple ignored the guns and dived to his knees, lifting Farge's head. There was a dull roaring in his ears and he saw the slack face of his friend through a mist of anguish. Dimly he heard the smaller FBI man's shaken yell.

"Tilly, he did the Dutch right in front of us. But what with, for hell's sake? I didn't hear any shot."

Lee Mason screamed again in a shrill, inhuman voice. "Grab that thing! It isn't a gun. It's a horrible new deadly weapon, a death ray, they've been working on. Get it before he uses it to kill us all."

Tillotson swore in a thick, stunned gasp and dived forward, grabbing the projector gingerly by its barrel. Rowe took an uncertain forward step, looking dazed, the pistol weaving in his hand.

At that precise moment Farge opened his eyes, smiled up at Curtis Temple and murmured, "Success!"

Temple was on his knees beside his friend. His lunge caught both

FBI men off balance and unprepared. His left hand closed on Tillotson's wrist and his right caught the butt of the projector and wrenched it free. Rowe was still swinging his pistol around when the firing stud clicked twice. Both men went down as if pole-axed. There had been no hum of power, no visible beam, but they lay unmoving.

Still yelping breathless shrieks, Lee Mason spun around and made a desperate leap for the door. With tight lips and cold eyes, Temple leveled the projector, centering it on the back of her head, and pressed the stud.

She stopped as if ramming an invisible wall. The echoes of an unfinished scream quivered in the air as her slim figure collapsed in the doorway.

On the tiny screen in front of Temple's eyes, a glowing ball of violet light flared up to almost intolerable brilliance for an instant and then vanished.

"Curt," Farge shouted, lurching to his feet. "You killed it! You destroyed it instantly. I saw it with my naked eye. It was like a little cloud of glowing mist that puffed out of her hair and whipped away to nothing. Curt, we've won!"

Temple was bending over Lee, feeling a surge of unutterable joy as he saw the rise and fall of her breast and felt the strong, steady beat of her pulse. He snatched the silver cap from the bench and fitted it down over the golden hair.

"We've won two tickets to the electric chair if we aren't long gone before those two Federal men wake up," he said. "Grab the projector and come on. We're about to add stealing government property to the list of our crimes."

A powerful sedan stood in the driveway, its engine idling softly. They scrambled in, with Temple at the wheel and Lee's limp figure propped between them. He stepped on the gas and the sedan whipped around in a tight, grinding turn. Its speedometer needle was at fifty and climbing when the narrow winding road plunged into the inky blackness of pine forest and Temple was forced to turn on the lights.

"Where do we go from here?" Farge asked. "The first thing those two do will be to set off a nationwide manhunt for us."

Temple chuckled thinly. "Not quite the first thing, Al. The first thing, thanks to Lee, will be to stumble through ten or fifteen miles of black woods to find a telephone. By that time we ought to be halfway to the Kansas line."

"You're—you're heading back to the camp?"

"Where else? We've got the detector and we've got the weapon. The only thing we don't have is any more time. That has just about run out—for us or for the entities."

Between them Lee Mason stirred and opened her eyes. For a moment she blinked dazedly, then gasped with the return of awareness. She flung herself against Temple, clutching his arm, sobbing, "Oh, Curt, I'm free I'm free! You wouldn't give up, even after all those horrible things I did to you."

He grinned, steering with one hand and using the other to give her shoulders a quick pressure. "You didn't do them, honey. It was that thing in your brain. But it's all over now and it can't ever happen again as long as you keep that silver cap on as a shield."

"I know, Curt. I—I watched you making it somewhere, way deep inside me, I was praying that I'd soon be wearing it." She whirled suddenly and threw her arms around the startled Farge. "But I wouldn't be if you weren't the bravest man and finest friend anyone ever had, Allen Farge. When you turned that projector on yourself, a part of me almost died for fear it might be too powerful."

Farge was beet red and stammering with embarrassment. "Now now, Miss Mason, I didn't do anything heroic. Curt is the one who has taken all the risks and is still taking them."

"I wish we could stop awhile and enjoy a real reunion," Temple said wistfully, "but that will have to wait. Right now we need to know every little thing you can tell us about those entities—what they are, where they came from, how they control so many people and what their real purpose is."

She sat up, frowning, and her lip quivered. "But that's the terrible part of it, Curt. I don't know. I—I can't answer a single one of your questions. You probably know more about those things right now than I do."

Temple took his eyes from the road long enough to throw her a startled, penetrating look. Farge was gaping at her openly.

"Let's take that from the beginning once more, a little slower this time so I can try to grasp it. Lee, you've been the mental and physical slave of those beings for more than a month, on the inside of everything that's occurred. There's even pretty strong evidence that you were a leader of the group."

She stared at him blankly. "Was I? All I really remember are bits and flashes of things that don't hitch together or make very much sense to me. Everything is clear enough up to the night we chipped through the covering on those meteorites. I remember a sharp pain in the back of my head and feeling dizzy. Then we all stood there, talking some kind of ridiculous gibberish for a few minutes. After that my memory seems to be all out of focus."

Temple pounded the wheel in impotent anger. "Of course. That damnable intelligence would take steps to guard against anyone's escaping with dangerous knowledge. In pioneer days Indians dragged a leafy branch behind them to wipe out their tracks. That's roughly what that thing must have done in your mind, Lee."

"We'd better have every scrap of what she does remember, Curt," Farge said. "That intelligence isn't perfect. We know hers made a couple of goofs. It might have accidentally let a fragment of important knowledge slip through without being fully erased."

"Yes," Lee said thoughtfully. "There were mistakes. I've forgotten what they were but I know they did happen. Part of it was trying to operate through imperfect human minds and bodies. It was a little like—like Heifitz trying to make a ten-dollar fiddle sound like a Stradivarius."

Temple grinned in spite of himself. "The dopey blob that let you wander off by yourself with a projector was no Heifitz, thank heaven. Go ahead, honey."

Dawn was breaking by the time Lee finished her scattered and misty recollections and slumped back in the seat, exhausted. Temple turned each disconnected item around in his mind, examining it from every angle without finding any hidden clue or fact of major significance. He glanced at Farge who shrugged and shook his head helplessly.

"I'm sorry," Lee said. "I wish I could help but everything is so confused and vague. I know I built projectors and helped design that rocket and its propulsion system, but not *consciously*. The real knowledge came *through* my brain, not out of it. I know quite a little about rocketry, but my own mind couldn't begin to understand what my hands were doing. Only once or twice, when I needed to solve smaller problems, I'd feel a sudden rush of energy, like an overdose of Benzedrine; my brain would race like crazy, and up would come the answer I needed."

Temple met Farge's look. "Pure mind energy, as we figured. How about your conversations? You must have had talks, discussions of projects."

"When we talked, it was just *us* talking. But I know those things had a way to communicate without us. Sometimes we'd all just stand or sit and I could feel thoughts flying. Then we'd all plunge into some new project. Once in a while words would pop into my mind and I'd say them to one of the others without knowing why. Sometimes I couldn't even understand what I was saying."

"Maybe," Farge said thoughtfully, "they were practicing or experimenting with our lower forms of thought and communication simply to discover what uses they could make of it. But you agree that Curt is right about the Crimson Plague? It's not a disease but a temporary condition they create for some purpose of their own?"

She shuddered. "Yes. That much I'm sure of, but what that purpose could be I haven't a ghost of memory. I only feel that it's something fantastic and utterly horrible."

They drove in silence for some time. Then Temple said, "The night I saw that first rocket launched, it went up a few miles, seemed to explode and completely vanished. I was frantic, wondering if it had blown up with you in it."

"They all do that," Lee said, and then started. "What made me say that? For a moment I almost recalled something."

"Think," Temple said sharply. "Think as hard as you can Lee, about the rocket ship. It started almost like a regular rocket, then vanished in a flash of light. Keep trying!"

"It's coming, Curt. Yes, the rocket has two propulsion systems. One is a very advanced development of our own rocket engines. That lifts it high enough so whatever happens when it shifts into another kind can't damage the camp. That's all I know, except that second stage is fast—faster than light. And coming back, it doesn't use the rocket at all. There's a flash of light and it just appears out of nowhere, sitting on its pad in the silo."

That was all she could tell them, despite a barrage of eager questions from both men. Temple said at last, "Okay, honey. But it looks to me as if there may be more memories only half buried that we can dredge up if we can figure out where to dig. Keep trying and tell us anything that pops into your mind."

The roadblock was waiting to trap them at the Kansas line. They saw it from some distance back—a highway patrol car parked crosswise, blocking half the road, a movable barricade across the remainder. Two state troopers got out of the car and stood in the road, waiting.

As Temple braked to a stop a few yards back, one of the troopers looked from their license plate to a paper in his hand and stiffened. He said something to his companion. Both dropped hands to their pistols and moved forward in a wary, stiff-legged stalk. Temple swung his door open and slid partway out, smiling pleasantly, waiting.

The two were separating to approach the car on both sides when he brought the projector up from his lap and pressed the stud. The troopers collapsed, as limp as rag dolls.

He jumped out, saw with relief that they were breathing shallowly and began to drag one toward their car. Farge and Lee jumped out to bring the other.

"Dump them in the back," Temple ordered, "then let the air out of all four tires. Unscrew the valves and throw them as far as you can.

We'll need every extra minute of time we can buy."

While Farge and Lee went at that task, he tore out the microphone of the police radio and hurled it into a clump of weeds, sending the ignition key after it. He reached behind the radio panel, jerked out a tangle of multicolored wires and threw them out into the field.

"I can just see the coroner's report on us," Farge said with grim humor. "Cause of death—compound fracture of the criminal laws. Anyhow, it's been nice knowing us."

They drove through, replaced the barricade and raced on, the speedometer quivering at ninety. Dusk was closing in when they neared the meteor camp turnoff to find the highway jammed with lines of slow-moving cars and the shoulders on both sides parked solid. Crowds stood by the parked cars, talking in low voices and watching the sky to the north.

Temple leaned out as they crept past one group. "What's all the excitement? What is everybody waiting for out here?"

"The big rocket," a man grunted. "Didn't you hear the news? They speeded up work and set the launching a full day ahead of schedule. It's blasting off at nine tonight with the first load of bodies for the moon."

Temple heard Lee gasp and Farge blurt a startled curse. He said grimly, "We can probably thank our success for that. Maybe they hoped to get off before we could start any more trouble. We haven't a moment to lose if we're to prevent their getting away with five hundred more helpless victims of their scheme."

But the highway was jammed and there was no place to pass or turn off. They could only sweat and fume while the traffic inched forward at an agonizing crawl. Where the road turned off to the camp they found the reason for the tie-up. A wooden barricade, illuminated by a row of flare-pots, barred the dirt road to the camp, and the gaunt figure of Gus Solle stood in front, waving a red lantern.

"Lee," Temple whispered urgently. "He might remember me from the night he picked up Mullane. You take over the wheel and turn in. He knows you and he may not have been alerted to your escape. Open your door so he can recognize you and call him over close."

Traffic was stationery at the moment. Temple scrambled over the back and crouched on the rear floor while Lee wriggled under the wheel. In a moment the car moved ahead and he felt it swing to the left. Gus Solle's nasal voice rose in a shout.

"Get back there, you! Can't you see this here barricade? Get back in line and keep going."

Lee's door opened, automatically switching on the dome light. In a cold voice she snapped, "Gus, you know me. It's Miss Mason and I

81

must get to the tower at once."

"I dunno." The voice sounded suspicious. "I was told not to let nobody in... *Say*, who's that next to you?"

"Come over here so I don't have to shout and I'll explain."

"No!" Solle's voice was shrill. "I'm staying right here until I get orders."

Temple raised up and triggered the projector. An entity in the act of leaving vanished in a soundless flash and Gus Solle collapsed, falling back out of sight among the weeds. It was over so swiftly that people in the cars might not have even noticed.

He sprang out and hurled the barricade off into the ditch. As he turned back he saw a few drivers leaning out, staring, and some men were running from parked cars. He waved his arms.

"Come along, everybody!" he bawled at the top of his lungs. "There's plenty of free parking right in front of the launch pad."

He sprang into the back and slammed the door. "Step on it, Lee. In about thirty seconds this road is going to turn into a drag strip for motorized lunatics and we'd better stay ahead of it. I only hope the sight of that mob of cars charging down on the camp gives those neon nasties something to think about besides us."

From behind rose a cacophony of blaring horns and clashing fenders as a stream of cars poured off the highway to follow them. He had a feeling that the entities would be more than a little distracted by the horde of uninvited spectators at his back. If they were to block the flight of the giant rocket, they would need plenty of diversion—and plenty of luck.

CHAPTER 13

Luck Runs Out

From where he and Farge crouched out of sight in the back of the sedan, Temple said softly, "You've got it straight now, Lee? Try to persuade the guard to shut off the current and open the gate for you. If we can get through without raising an alarm, we've got some chance of getting through to the rocket silo before the fighting starts. If we have to crash the gate, we face a pitched battle right there against pretty heavy odds."

"I'll do my best," Lee said. "Lord knows I had plenty of practice getting through. Quiet, now. I'm stopping at the gate."

She leaned out and motioned imperiously to the glaring guard inside. Her voice was coldly commanding. "Jonas, open the gate for me immediately. I have just escaped from kidnapers and I must report to the tower at once."

In the rear, Temple felt cold perspiration crawl down his face as he waited through a dragging silence. Then Lee's whisper came, ragged with strain. "Curt, he doesn't answer me or even move. He just stands there like a statue."

"Oh-oh!" Temple raised far enough to peer out through the detector and his face hardened. "I thought so. Two free entities are floating over to investigate. The one on his own skull is waiting for their report before it gives him his orders. Don't panic, sweet. I'll handle them."

The click of the projector was followed by two violet flashes on the detector screen. Instantly the guard yelled and started to run toward the gate controls and telephone in the shanty. A lance of invisible fury destroyed his guiding entity and sent him sprawling in the dust.

A spark of violet flicked across the detector screen and was gone, too fast for the eye to follow. Temple hurled the car door open and plunged out.

"Get out, quick! The fat's in the fire now. There was another of those things prowling and I didn't see it in time. It's gone to sound the alarm." He slid into the driver's seat. "Stand well back. All hell's going to break loose when this buggy hits that charged gate."

The engine roared and the heavy sedan shot backward. The first cars from the highway were just streaming over the rise when he reversed and shoved his foot to the floor boards. The car hurtled back down the gentle slope straight at the gate, its thunder rising to a howl.

At the last possible moment Temple forced the door open, steadied the wheel, flipped the automatic transmission to neutral and jumped. Arms folded over his face, he struck the soft ground with stunning force and rolled. An instant later the heavy car, its momentum unchecked, smashed into the charged gate.

There was a rending crash and crackle, a blaze of greenish flame and the alarm bells set up their harsh clangor. With the wrecked gate folded around it, the car slewed around and crashed into the guard shanty.

As it collapsed, there was a smaller crackle of sparks from the gate control panel, the bells stopped jangling and every light in the camp winked out. A moment later dim lights winked on along the streets and the bells resumed their yammering. Obviously the entities had learned a lesson from Temple's previous invasion and had installed an auxiliary lighting system to take over if the main line blew out.

Temple staggered to his feet, stunned and bruised but not seriously injured. Lee and Farge ran up, white-faced. "Curt, are you all right? You might have been killed, jumping at that speed."

"I'm fine." He snatched the detector and projector he had left with Lee for safekeeping. "You two stay outside. You wouldn't stand a chance in there unarmed and you'd only handicap me."

"Who's unarmed?" Farge growled. He charged in past the tangled wreck of gate and car, rolled the guard's body over and drew a projector from under it. "I spotted this in his belt. Give me five seconds and I'll have it converted into an entity-destroyer."

"I'm going with you," Lee said flatly. "I still remember the layout of the camp pretty well and I may see other things that will bring back some memories."

There was no time to argue. "Stay behind me and spread out. The big rocket's our target number one. We can't let that blast off with its human cargo."

Beyond the fence, cars were piling up and voices were yelling. Temple ignored them and ran down the street toward the tower, the others at his heels. Ahead, a knot of armed guards burst into sight, racing toward them. Probably, Temple thought, they had been pulled off fence duty to handle some important task connected with the rocket.

Guns blazed and lead hissed and whined around the trio, or kicked spurts of dust from the street. Temple snapped the projector but apparently the range was too great for effect.

"Take cover," he panted over his shoulder. "I'll zigzag forward until I can knock them out with the beam."

His head was jerking crazily as he tried to search the air through the detector screen and still keep an eye on the guards. He saw three of the violet blobs whipping toward him in a cluster, with a number of others spread out behind. A single burst destroyed the three and the rest fled.

Lead was singing all around him. Only his evasive action and the difficulty of aiming on the dead run kept him from being riddled. Then he saw a guard drop to one knee and take careful aim. The range still seemed too great but in desperation he triggered the projector, sweeping it in an arc. The kneeling rifleman toppled and the front rank of runners melted so swiftly that those behind tripped over them.

Yelling exultantly, Temple sprayed the invisible beam over the melee and was exhilarated by the dazzling burst of violet flashes. Every guard was down, their limp figures sprawled in a bloodless comic-opera grotesquerie of mock carnage. As he ran past the tumbled bodies, he was suddenly aware that Lee and Farge had never run to cover but faced the gunfire with him.

Farge paused to rummage over the fallen guards, then ran to catch up. "Guns, but not a projector in the lot."

"There aren't many," Lee panted. "I remember, we could only make a few crystals at a time. We were too busy."

"Make?" Temple cried over his shoulder. "Do you mean those are synthetics, made from materials right here on Earth?"

Lee nodded. "But don't ask me what materials."

There was no more human interference, no visible sign of hovering entities as they burst into the open space at the foot of the rocket tower. Lee motioned. "Around this way. There's a door that leads straight to the rocket's loading ramp."

They swerved to the right, took a dozen pounding strides. In the lead Temple stiffened and skidded to a stop, hands half lifted, eyes wide in an incredulous stare. The others stopped beside him, gaping.

Before their bulging eyes rose a second tower, immensely larger than the first, a quarter mile to the north. The central tower, directly in line with the gate, had masked it from their view before.

"Curt," Lee cried. "I can't remember ever seeing that second tower before."

"It's new," Temple said bitterly. "I'm the world's prize knuckle-head. I never stopped to think that their new giant rocket would require a new giant launching tower of its own. It's from there, not here, that another five hundred helpless victims are about to be shot to the moon."

"There might still be time to stop it," Farge said. "That street runs straight through to…" His words trailed off as a faint rumble made the air and earth quiver.

At the open top of the tower a faint glow appeared and grew swiftly brighter as the sound and vibration rose. The sound became a titanic, howling thunder and the monstrous new rocket burst from its silo. Up and up it fled, hurling its trail of intolerable flame, and vanished in a soundless flash as it shifted to the new drive; perhaps, Temple thought, to a new dimension. Afterward the invisible storm of ionized air or whatever swept them eerily and was gone.

The spell was broken by sudden movement from the deep shadows, the wink of light on metal. Temple yelled and spun around. His outflung arms caught the others and sent them reeling back an instant before the pale blue beam flicked past. He triggered the projector at the shadows. There was a flash of violet light and the body of another guard pitched into the street.

Farge ran to snatch up his fallen projector. He worked at it for a moment, with a tiny pocket screwdriver, then handed it to Lee with a flourish. "You now have your own projector. Welcome to the club."

Temple was standing in an attitude of hopeless dejection, his head still thrown back, eyes staring bleakly at the sky. By their failure, five hundred more human beings had been hurled from the familiar Earth toward unknowable anguish on an alien world. They, and all the others before them, were beyond reach of any human aid. How many so-called Crimson Plague victims had already been sent to the moon? Five thousand? Ten?

Suddenly he tensed with a startled exclamation that brought the others spinning around. "What is it, Curt? I can't see anything."

He gestured upward. "Entities—thousands of them. They're pouring in from every direction, diving into the top of this smaller tower above us like swallows returning to their chimney at sundown."

"Maybe—" Farge began, then yelled and pointed.

A small, slim figure had burst from the base of the great rocket tower and was running furiously, desperately, up the wide street toward the smaller tower beside them. As it burst through the glow of an auxiliary street lamp, Temple recognized the thin, pale face with its line of neat black mustache.

"Rocky," he cried. "It's Dr. Eno Rocossen."

The little physicist was clutching a projector and running as if his life depended upon it. In that moment of startled recognition, Temple saw a whole knot of men burst from the larger tower to follow at the same frantic run.

He gasped with the shock of recognition at the same moment Lee cried, "Curt, it's the whole Meteoritics Team. There's Jacobs, Spirovic, Bensil, all of them." A big blond man, a total stranger to Temple, ran through the light and she added. "And Mr. Van Arden of NASA."

Temple had completely forgotten the man whose early morning phone call had plunged him into this nightmare. But there were more

86

important matters to face now. Every member of the group was carrying a weapon of some kind.

He glimpsed three or four blue beam projectors, several guns, clubs. He took it for granted that they were charging to attack the three intruders. Then realization burst upon him.

"They aren't after us. They're heading for the smaller rocket, just as all those entities were, evacuating their base here on Earth. You said Rocky was pilot of the small rocket. He's flying them all back to the moon, beyond our reach."

"Good riddance," Farge said, his eyes shining. "We've licked 'em, Curt, chased them and their dirty business off the Earth."

"No," Temple cried. "If they get away, we're whipped. They can stay there, out of reach, with an army of mindless slaves until they've built up a new plan of conquest. We've got to stop them. That rocket is our only hope of blocking them and saving those thousands of poor victims they kidnapped. Come on!"

Rocossen, still running at his furious pace, was almost to the tower where they stood in the shadows, the other scientists only yards behind him. In the detector screen they showed as a swarm of bobbing violet fireflies.

Temple burst from the shadows, running to intercept the physicist, lifting the projector. He saw Rocossen's eyes widen, his stride falter at the first shock of surprise. Then his own projector flashed up and the trigger studs clicked in unison.

The blue beam missed by no more than an inch as Temple flung himself aside. But the movement evidently spoiled his own aim, since there was no violet flash of a disintegrating entity. Before he could aim again, Rocossen darted aside and raced toward a smaller door, barely visible in the tower base. Temple pounded after him, centering his projector with cold deliberation. Behind him rose Lee's clear cry. "Destroy it, Curt! His is one of the most powerful and dangerous entities of all."

On the detector screen the thing seemed huge, its violet hue deeper and richer. As Rocossen fumbled with the door, Temple had a clear point-blank shot. His finger pressed the firing stud.

In the same instant, his reflex jerked the projector up so the invisible destroying force whipped harmlessly over its target. At the same moment, Rocossen jerked the door open and darted inside.

Farge, pounding up, gasped, "You missed, Curt. You had a clear shot and something jerked your arm."

"I jerked it," Temple panted. "That rocket's the only hope of escape for those poor devils on the moon. If I destroyed his entity, Rocky wouldn't know how to fly it, and neither would we. I've got to grab him with that thing still alive and somehow force it to obey our orders.

You and Lee block the door, try to hold the others back until I grab him. Use your projectors on them."

Without waiting for an answer he plunged into the shadowy interior of the tower. The smaller rocket, still immense, loomed over him, its nose hidden in the shadowy upper reaches of the tower. He saw that it crouched in a deep pit, a full third of its body below ground level. Straight ahead a wide gangplank led across the outer edge of that pit to an open port in the side of the rocket. The port lock, hinged at the bottom, stood out to form a platform on which the far end of the gangplank rested.

Light flooded from the rocket's interior onto the figure of Rocossen staggering breathlessly across the gangplank. Behind him Temple heard yells and the sound of conflict as the entity-driven mob hurled itself on Lee and Farge. He wanted desperately to look around, to check on their safety, but there was not a second to be spared. He hurled himself onto the gangplank, shouting "*Rocky*! Stop or I'll use the destroying beam."

On the port threshold, Rocossen whirled around and the blue beam lashed out. Temple felt a stab of excruciating agony and his whole right side went numb. His leg crumpled and he pitched down, landing with head and shoulders out over the edge. The projector flew from his paralyzed hand to crash onto the concrete floor a full fifty feet below.

Rocossen had darted into the rocket and disappeared. Gasping, trembling, Temple hauled himself back from the edge just as machinery inside the ship began to whine. Hydraulic pistons set up a rhythmic, gurgling thudding and under him the gangplank began to quiver.

The port lock was rising, closing, lifting the end of the gangplank with it. In a matter of moments the rising lock would slip completely out from under the end of the plank, letting it plunge into the pit with Temple still on it. If by a miracle he survived the fall, he would be directly under the blast tubes of the rocket, trapped in a pocket of seething flames.

Cold sweat blinded him as he scrabbled with left arm and leg to force himself up the gangplank. The steepening angle added to his problem but he gritted his teeth and inched forward. He was almost to the port, near enough to see that the area of overlap under the gangplank had dwindled to a hair. At any instant the rising lock would slip past the end, and he still had an agonizing two feet to cover. He would never make it…

CHAPTER 14

On The Moon

Running steps clattered up the gangplank. Strong hands grabbed hold of his jacket and Temple felt himself lifted, dragged and literally flung over the rim of the lock. He slid and rolled down the steep incline to the floor, hearing the far-off clatter of the dislodged gangplank crashing into the pit.

A body came tumbling down, landing across his legs. Lee Mason, her golden hair disheveled, grinned at him with bruised lips and murmured, "Just made it, darling."

Above them the port lock chugged into its seal and almost instantly the rocket quivered to the first murmur of awakening blasts. Temple cried wildly, "Lee! How...? What are you doing in here?"

"I saw you about to take a dive and ran to help you in," she panted. "Allen stayed behind to hold them back. He caught a paralysis beam and lost his projector, but he's doing all right with one fist. At least we're together, Curt dear."

The mounting thunder of the rockets penetrated his daze and an expression of frantic anguish twisted his face. "He's blasting off. We've got to stop him. We'll be killed, crushed to a pulp by the acceleration."

It was too late. The floor lurched under them, then an irresistible force smashed down with crushing pressure. Through a mist of agony Temple glimpsed Lee's face, contorted almost beyond recognition by the terrible forces of acceleration. Then a wave of blackness swept over his senses.

Consciousness rushed back over him in a wave. His whole body felt as if he had been beaten with clubs. A sharp tingling in his right arm and leg told him the effects of the paralysis beam were wearing off. The rockets had been cut off and there was no sound or sensation of movement whatever.

He found he could move his head and rolled it, fighting a numbing fear for Lee Mason's safety. She lay beside him and the regular movement of her breast told him she was alive. At the same moment he saw what had saved them. The floor on which they lay had seemed iron-hard but he saw now that it was actually a firmly resilient plastic of some unfamiliar kind. It had yielded to the press of their bodies, cushioning them against the worst fury of acceleration.

With tremendous effort he forced himself to a sitting position. Suddenly there was a lurch that brought a wave of nausea to the pit of his stomach. A thin, high whine wracked his eardrums. The very air around him quivered with a vibration that made everything waver, as if he were viewing the interior of the rocket through heat waves.

As suddenly as they began, the effects vanished. His vision had never seemed so clear, his whole being so exhilarated. Beside him, Lee Mason sat up, wide-eyed. "What happened, Curt? I suddenly feel wonderful but strange."

"I think we just slipped into that hyper-drive or dimensional drive or space-warp, whatever it is. If you're all right, I'll go up forward and give Rocky the shock of his life. I don't believe he realized he was carrying passengers this trip."

"I'll go with you. Curt, what are we going to do next? We can't fight an army of controlled slaves on the moon. You seem to have lost your projector and I gave mine to Allen."

Temple shrugged helplessly. "Play it by ear, I guess. We can't jump out and walk back so we'll just have to follow through."

To his surprise he found gravity normal, probably maintained by artificial means. If by chance they should survive and win this fantastic war, there were enough secrets in this ship alone to advance terrestrial space science a hundred years in one leap. At the moment, he thought dismally, the survival chances were extremely slim.

They crept along a narrow corridor, lined with closed sliding doors. Walls and ceiling were covered with a black, tar-like substance that resembled the meteorites as he had studied them through glasses. It was probably the same cosmic ray shield that had enabled the entities to survive the journey through space.

At the end of the corridor they peered cautiously into the control room of the rocket. Temple's breath caught, not at the intricacy but at the simplicity of the layout. He had expected a bailing maze of weird and unfamiliar instruments. Instead, Rocossen lay in a massively padded reclining seat before a panel that bore a single dial, four snap switches and one movable control knob. Apparently the operation from blast-off to landing was almost entirely automated.

In front of him a large television screen was filled with a color image of the moon with the massive crater of Plato in the exact center. Every detail stood out in breathtaking, almost three-dimensional clarity. Temple could pick out the nearby craters of Eudoxis and Cassini and identify the individual peaks of the great saw-toothed mountain ranges. The weird, unexplained colors in the depths of Plato were faintly diffused, indicating the presence of some form of atmosphere. A smaller screen bore a receding image of Earth, dimly lit and red-haloed.

Rocossen stirred, turned his head and saw them. His mouth flew open and his eyes went wide. "You! I thought you were both finished, or at least stopped."

"Sorry to disappoint you, Rocky," Temple said dryly, "but the opportunity to visit the moon was irresistible."

"It is better this way," Rocossen said, relaxing. "Now the great Monj himself will be able to watch the removal of your annoying plate and the occupation of your brain. There is knowledge there we need and it has already been too long withheld."

"Monj?" Temple said. "Who in the devil…?"

"Monj, the Master of the Moon," Rocossen said, drawing himself stiffly upright on the seat. "Our great leader whose intelligence planned and directed our project." He snatched a projector from his belt and leveled it, his eyes alight with malicious triumph. "This time I'll make sure that you are in no condition to cause trouble when you confront Monj."

Lee gasped sharply. Temple suddenly yawned with elaborate nonchalance, leaned against the bulkhead and casually examined his own fingernails. "If this ship is insulated against cosmic rays, then it must also keep out all less powerful radiations as well. Tell me, old boy, where is that trinket going to collect the energy its crystal is supposed to concentrate into a paralysis beam?"

The expression on Rocossen's face was ludicrous in its dawning comprehension. In a pleasant, conversational voice, Temple drawled, "It looks as if you chaps goofed again, doesn't it?"

The little physicist snarled a curse and hurled the projector at Temple's head. It bounced off the bulkhead as Rocossen exploded from the seat and threw himself onto Temple, hitting, kicking, clawing like a wildcat. They went to the floor in a savage, struggling tangle. Temple had his hands full simply keeping his face away from those clawed hands.

"Try to hold him still until I can slug him with this, Curt." Lee was circling, waving a silver pocket flask. "I didn't want to risk damaging the projector so I went hunting for a club. One of the Plague victims back there had this in his pocket."

"Is there anything in it?" Temple panted.

"It's full." She twisted the cap and sniffed. "Whiskey. But this is no time…"

With a furious effort, Temple got the squirming Rocossen pinned down and held out his hand. "Hand it to me with the cap off."

As Lee gaped he began pouring liquor into Rocossen's mouth, pinching his nostrils to make him swallow. He grinned up at her. "It

91

just occurred to me than an entity would have a jolly time trying to control a brain buzzing with alcohol fumes. As I remember, two drinks had Rocky climbing the wall."

In the battered detector screen he caught a glimpse of the violet blob jerking free and darting erratically off down the corridor. Beneath him Rocossen's struggling figure went limp. He got to his feet, panting from the exertion of the struggle.

The little physicist shuddered, opened bleary eyes, hiccupped and sat up. "Curtish! And Mish Mashon! You free me from my shameful bondage. Wordsh can never expresh my appre—appre—my gratitude. Oh, to think that I, a Doctor of Philosliophy and Fellof of the Royal Shoshiety, would be forshed to do horrible, shameful—" He put his face in his hands and sobbed.

"Don't let it break you up, Rocky," Temple said, winking at Lee. "You had plenty of distinguished company in your life of shame. Our job now is to see that it doesn't recur."

Rocossen lifted an angry, tear-streaked face. "Wait till I get my handsh on that Monj, Mashter of the Moon. I'll kill the shon of a bish."

"And I'll probably let you," Temple said. "First we have to figure how to keep ourselves alive and get at him."

"Curt!" Lee clutched his arm. "We forgot something. You've driven out his controlling entity. What if he can't remember how to land the rocket?"

Rocossen lurched to his feet. "No problem at all, Mish Mashon. 'Sh'all automatic." He blinked owlishly up at the viewscreen. "In fact, we've already landed."

Temple whirled and gaped at the screen. The image of the moon had been replaced by that of a great vaulted cavern, with a lighted tunnel in the center of the screen. He whirled and thrust the half-empty flask into Lee's hand.

"Bottoms up, sweet. Down this to the last delicious drop."

"Me? But why?"

"Because, my girl, otherwise the first thing they'll do out there is yank off your silver cap and take over your brain again, and I'd rather save the rest of our battles until after we're married." He swung around to the other. "You've made this trip often enough, Rocky. What will we be facing out there?"

"Slaves—hundreds of poor, helplesh devils like myshelf. Huge, glowing caverns. Mines that go almost down to the shenter of the moon. Ugly monsters like nothing you ever shaw, even in a nightmare. And thoushands of those things hovering in the air. I never saw 'em but I could feel their intelligence flowing all around me."

Temple shuddered. "A delightful picture of our hosts but not of our future. But I guess we haven't much choice."

"Curtis!" Rocossen staggered against him, clawing at his arm. "You're not going out there to face *them*? You can't! You don't know the fearful danger." Shock was sobering him rapidly but Temple hoped enough fumes would remain in his brain to provide immunity for at least a time.

"If we don't face them now," he said somberly, "we may have to later as conquerors of the Earth. Now that they know how, it shouldn't be hard for them to launch more shielded meteorites with enough entities to take over. And they have the big rocket to haul an army of controlled slaves." He frowned at Lee who was choking on the last of the liquor. "I hope that doesn't hit you the way it did Rocky."

She grinned. "Wel-l-l, I won't say I'm exactly hilariously happy, but on the other hand I'm not afraid of the big bad moon wolf any more. Shall we go before that feeling wears off?"

CHAPTER 15

The Vards

The port lock finished opening and the trio stared out into a tunnel, brightly lit by banks of glowing rods in the ceiling. It appeared to be empty, but Temple's detector screen showed entities hovering in a watchful cloud some distance back.

As they stepped from the rocket, Temple saw that what had appeared to be a tunnel was actually a telescoping metal tube, extended to form an airtight seal around the port. In tense silence they walked forward, alert for attack that failed to come. There was no sign of visible life as far as they could see.

Abruptly the passage turned and opened into a great vaulted cavern, completely lined with the black shielding substance. All along one side massive machines of unfamiliar design and unknown purpose hummed quietly behind low metal screens. Beyond, a broad passage slanted steeply downward, reminding Temple of Rocossen's babble about mines in the center of the moon.

Opposite, a closed door was set into the wall, and beside it hung six objects that could only be space suits meant for human beings or creatures of human form. They were constructed of an unfamiliar metal, with oxygen tanks and bulbous, transparent helmets.

Temple studied them blankly, gave up and shifted his gaze. A deep shadowy alcove seemed to be filled with odd doll-like objects. He started, then gulped at the realization that they were unrevived Plague bodies, standing in rows like logs on end.

A gasp from Lee brought his head around and for the first time he saw the three living men. The one in the center, tall and gaunt, bore the most vivid and gigantic entity his detector had ever revealed. He did not need Rocossen's awed whisper to know that he was face to face with Monj, Master of the Moon.

But what wrung a gasp of stunned incredulity from his lips was the circle of monstrous shapes that came slithering out of the shadows on both sides to surround them. Lee's fingers went tight on his arm, pressing with unconscious ferocity. Rocossen gasped, "The Vards!"

They were like grotesque sea monsters out of their element, each a travesty of a terrestrial octopus but with ten great tentacles on which they shuffled awkwardly. Leathery, bulbous bodies tapered to a rounded top that apparently constituted the head. Four huge, round, black eyes were spaced equally around this protrusion, enabling the creature to see in every direction without the need of a flexible neck.

Four of the tentacles, thicker than the rest, terminated in round sucker discs that served as feet. The six remaining tentacles were slimmer and terminated in both a row of smaller discs and waving tendrils that seemed to perform the function of fingers.

Horrible as they appeared, Temple got a sudden strong impression that they were neither hostile nor willfully evil. The great saucer eyes were intelligent, even sad. Then he saw the glowing entity perched on each head and realized with a shock that these, too, were slaves of the mind-energy beings.

In that moment his understanding of the entities broadened. Because they were mind energy, expressing themselves through the minds of hosts they commanded, only the most intelligent could be used. On Earth they had taken full control of only the best-trained scientific minds, indicating a need for already established thought patterns. Those incapable of absorbing the extra burst of mind energy to useful purpose became mere controlled dupes.

These Vards, then, must be creatures endowed with the needed intelligence to begin with. Watching the movements of those prehensile tentacles, Temple realized how the nebulous beings must have used that dexterity to build this base and to construct the "meteorites" that bombarded Kansas.

Lee pressed against him, shuddering. "Curt, do you suppose they were original natives of the moon, enslaved by these things?"

"I don't think so, Lee. These Vards, as Rocossen called them, don't appear to have the necessary physical adaptation to lunar extremes of heat and cold. Also, they seem to be oxygen breathers since they show no discomfort from the air here, which feels very much like the atmosphere we're accustomed to. But we'll probably find out all about them, and matters more unpleasant, almost immediately."

His detector showed the vaulted ceiling of the great chamber literally jammed with solid masses of the hovering beings. Their numbers must run into the tens of thousands, he thought hopelessly, forming a concentration of malignant intelligence beyond comprehension. Against them stood three puny humans, only one of whom could even see the enemy.

Apparently in response to a silent command the semicircle of Vards began shuffling forward, closing their ranks and irresistibly forcing the trio closer to Monj and his two companions.

Rocossen turned a pale, strained face toward Temple and whispered, "Oh, Lord, to think that only a short time ago I was actually trafficking with these unholy monsters. After you freed me by driving

95

that thing out of my brain I remembered the Vards, but only vaguely. I didn't realize how hideous they are until I see them now with my normal senses."

The gaunt figure that was the vehicle for Monj opened its mouth and a booming voice rolled forth. "Silence! Slaves do not whisper, or even dare to speak without permission, in the presence of the Master of the Moon." The supreme arrogance of that command reached down inside Temple and rasped on nerves already raw from strain, worry and fear. A blinding, heedless anger swept over him, smothering caution.

"Oh, shut up!" he shouted furiously. "Who are you to be giving orders to your betters? You're nothing but a cheap parasite who couldn't wipe its own nose without its slavey. In our league you couldn't even be master of mud balls. We aren't your slaves and never will be. You thought you could conquer and rule Earth but you're looking at three people you can't control, and we're going to cross your wires and blow your fuse."

The echoes of his wrath died away. Lee and Rocossen were staring at him in shocked horror. The Vards were quivering nervously, and overhead the swarms of entities milled like disturbed bees. As his rage faded, even Temple was shocked at his own outburst. He expected an outburst of fury, physical violence—anything but the reaction he got.

The voice of Monj sounded genuinely puzzled. "Invade and rule Earth? Why should we want to do that? We don't want that poor, sterile globe you dwell upon. What possible satisfaction or glory could we find in ruling a race whose most intelligent life-forms are little more than primitive savages in comparison to our vast knowledge?" Temple's jaw dropped. In some incomprehensible way, Monj's words carried conviction. Against his will and against all reason, he found himself believing the unbelievable. In the space of the same heartbeat, he realized that to admit his feeling would be to weaken his own position.

He snapped, "When you were hard up for knowledge, I notice it was those same 'primitive savages' you raided to get it. And if what you did wasn't invasion, or that Crimson Plague swindle conquest, it was a mighty realistic imitation. Personally, I think you're a pack of cheap parasites who got kicked out of a civilized world as mental delinquents. You go around leeching onto the output of real brains and claiming it as your own."

A wave of anger crossed the face of Monj, to be replaced by calm deliberation. After a silence, he nodded. "Yes, I realize our action could be misinterpreted. You are one of the more intelligent specimens of your race, and also our most serious obstacle. The female, there, was important to us, as was the other, who operated the rocket, but you wrested them both from our control. Perhaps knowing the truth would

96

make you less dangerous to us. Your reactions might even provide us an unexpected clue. Relax and let your minds receive thought patterns. It is swifter and more sure than your crude method of communicating by noises of the mouth. Do not be afraid. You will be quite safe until you have heard our story through."

Into Temple's stunned mind came weird, incredible scenes, vividly real, stirring his emotions. As they flashed by, a soft disembodied voice explained in running commentary. By the awed expressions on the faces of Lee and Rocossen he knew they, too, were sharing the same experience.

The images swept him up across space, past worlds, stars, systems, galaxies to a place beyond the horizon of even man's knowledge. "A world called Xacrn, which is a planet in the system of the faint star you call Seventeen Leporis," the voice murmured. "We are Xacrns, ultimate evolutionary forms of the highest life order in the cosmos. Once, a million generations past, we possessed physical bodies more useful and adaptable than yours."

Temple saw Vards tilling alien fields, fabricating strange and intricate tools with those delicate tentacle tips, building magnificent cities. "Inevitably, some were interested only in developing only their minds, more hungry for knowledge than for physical possessions. It is always thus with every race. Even on your world, the gap between farmer and scholar widens.

"As ages passed our separate interests evolved divergent body-forms. The Vards, content to blend artistry with knowledge, were little changed. We, who ignored our bodies to fill our minds, found our physical structures sloughed off, discarded by the relentless sweep of evolution."

Like time-lapse photographs, the scenes condensed endless millennia into nightmare visions of tentacles, withered from disuse, falling away, of bodies wasting to dust until nothing remained but the glowing clouds of pure mind energy.

"Take heed, you of Earth," the voice thundered. "Your evolution may one day carry you to the same ultimate state. Already, in a mere hundred of your years, you have seen your sturdy bodies weaken as your minds grew stronger. Unless you stop before it is too late, you will some day become like us."

Temple felt a wave of horror. The logic in that prophecy was inescapable. While American science and knowledge leaped ahead at an accelerating pace, the physical condition of its populace was already a matter of grave concern.

The scenes flashed from the drifting entities to the normal Vards, content to labor and prosper. The voice seemed to grow more arrogant.

"When we had acquired all the knowledge of our world we turned to the system, then the galaxy. The Vards gave us the physical bodies and skills and served as our corporeal vehicles, while we gave them access to our vast knowledge. It was a most happy partnership for both."

Yeah, Temple thought dryly, *I'll bet the Vards were overjoyed at becoming mindless slaves.* He started when the voice said stiffly, "They were honored to be so favored." He could not be sure the words were a direct answer to his thoughts but the possibility was disturbing.

"Too late we realized our own doom," the narrative continued. "The doom of perfection. We overlooked the fact that while evolution may be speeded, slowed or diverted into strange by-paths, as your scientists have done through radiation bombardment, it cannot be halted. What we had thought was our ultimate energy-form was not the ultimate after all. Ahead lay one more step—the merging of our separate identities into the one great, all-pervading universal energy—for us, oblivion." The voice fell to a note of ineffable sadness. "In a few hundred generations we, the highest life-form in the cosmos, will cease to exist." Temple saw tears sparkle in Lee's eyes, felt his own throat tighten. "We refused to submit to our doom. Somewhere in the universe there must be a key to the salvation of our race. A great ship was built and I was commissioned to find it."

On the screen of his mind Temple followed the endless search through the reaches of space, from world to world and system to system. He saw it come at last to our solar system and flash toward Earth. He could almost feel the tearing impact of the wandering meteorite that smashed the controls and sent it crashing into the Plato crater on the dead moon.

"We lived in the wrecked ship until those Vards who survived could construct this haven. We were beyond the limits of our communication so we could not even call to our world for rescue. We began to construct crude vessels and hurl them toward your world. Strangely in one spot on Earth, and only one, there is a supply of an element also found on Xacrn. We had only to use material of the opposite magnetic property and the vehicles were drawn to that spot without the need for guidance systems."

An Earth element similar to one on Xacrn, and found only one place on Earth? Temple's eyes widened and he almost shouted, "*Helium!* The only known deposits of helium in any sizable quantity are in Kansas. You just shot off the stones and the helium pockets under Kansas drew them down like magnets."

"Of course. But it was a long time before we realized that the voyagers were destroyed on the way by radiations in space. Protected by

98

the shielding in our wrecked ship, we had been unaware of such a menace, and we were facing a disaster of another kind. Our Vards, being mortal, were growing old and weak and were dying off quickly. Soon we would be left stranded and utterly helpless.

"With almost their last strength, our surviving Vards built the new vehicles and shielded them with material from the ship. This time the expedition survived to build the crude rocket ships and establish communications, as you have seen."

In Temple's mind, the screen went blank as the picture story ended. For a full minute he was too stunned to marshal his surging thoughts. He drew a ragged breath.

"Now that you've done it, what have you gained? If you had no intention of taking over our world, what were you—or are you—really after? You've told me everything but the one basic fact."

"That," Monj said coldly, "will be revealed to you when you become a part of our project."

The words jerked Temple back to the harsh realities of their position. "If you wait for that, you'll be as dead as your Vards and from the same cause—old age."

"You underestimate me, Dr. Temple." He waved a hand toward Lee and Farge. "Remove their protective caps and hold them until the fumes in their brains have evaporated sufficiently for us to resume control. Have this one prepared for an immediate operation."

"Operation?" The word burst out of Temple in a croak.

The figure of Monj held up slim hands. "This body and brain were the property of a skilled surgeon. They will have no difficulty in removing your silver plate and substituting one of a less troublesome metal so that you may apply your full abilities to the furtherance of our work." He motioned to a Vard. "Get the operating table and instruments ready at once."

The grotesque creature bowed, opened a triangular mouth and said in perfect English, "It shall be done as ordered, Master."

The shock of hearing human speech from that alien mouth held Temple and his companions frozen, gaping. In that moment the remaining Vards closed in. Leathery tentacles whipped around them, pinning their arms from shoulder to wrist. A tentacle reached to pluck the detector from Temple's forehead.

The prospect of losing his last slender advantage filled him with desperation. In a frenzy of resistance he jerked his head back from the reaching tendrils and fought with new fury to free himself. Muscles swelled and corded, sweat streamed down his face as he writhed and strained.

Suddenly, incredibly, one of the sucker discs let go with a *pop* like a drawn champagne cork, then another and another. He felt tentacles slipping. It seemed incredible, impossible, but he was slowly winning his trial of strength with the giant decapods. The explanation exploded in his mind.

"Fight them," he panted. "Monj said the Vards were dying of old age, with barely strength enough left to send those meteorites. Keep resisting. Wear them down."

He could hear Monj raging. The detector showed entities streaming down into the alcove to seize and revive the army of human bodies. With a superhuman surge of effort Temple tore away the last tentacle and broke free.

Lee and Farge were struggling furiously. Temple plunged to their aid, prying sucker discs loose, dragging the tentacles from their waning grip. The last strength seemed to drain out of the great Vards swiftly and in moments he had the other two freed, if their perilous situation could be considered freedom. Human figures were running from the alcove, spurred by the controlling entities. They were young, strong, invincible.

"Outside," Temple panted, "It's our only escape. I'll try to hold them off while you and Lee get into those space suits."

"No," Rocossen said. "Grab suits and run out. We can put them on out there. I remember, there's enough thin air to sustain us a few minutes."

Then the theory held by many astronomers was true, that the moon did retain some thin atmosphere with the heavier molecules trapped in pools in the depths of the giant craters. Even a little would temper the intense cold and give them precious moments to don the space suits. No entity would dare leave the shielded cavern to pursue them into the bombardment of cosmic rays.

An idea flamed in Temple's mind. In midstride he swerved and caught the limp tentacles of the Vard leader, who had slumped to the floor, exhausted by the struggle. Without pausing he raced on, dragging the unresisting creature with him.

Lee was jerking suits from the wall while Rocossen struggled with the door catch. Temple snatched a suit and followed into a small air lock, slamming the inner door in the face of pursuit. A blast of intense cold struck him as the outer door swung open.

Not daring to waste breath on speech, they stumbled across an expanse of what seemed to be a lava shell toward a jumbled heap of gray rock. High above them, sunlight threw a knife-edged lance of almost intolerable illumination along the top of the crater wall, but in the crater it was intensely dark. Only a faint reflection caught by the tenuous atmosphere gave them enough light to see where they were going.

As they struggled into the bulky suits and clamped down the bulbous helmets, fresh invigorating air poured over them. The sounds of gasping breaths and a muttered exclamation sounded in Temple's ears. He said, "Well, what do you know? These have some kind of intercom system."

"Why, they do," Lee said. Then her voice sharpened. "Curt, what a cruel thing to do, dragging that poor creature out here without protection. It can't survive."

"I'm pretty sure it can, Lee. They had to work in the open to build that immense layout and to launch the meteorites, and I can't quite visualize a space suit to fit them. If I'm right, it will have knowledge we'll need to survive. It should be a willing ally, since it was a slave of the entities, too."

The Vard stirred and sat up. Its voice came clearly. "You are correct, Dr. Temple. We feel no cold and our enormous lungs find oxygen even in the thinnest air. I do thank you for my freedom. It is a new and frightening feeling, but I believe I like it."

Lee's voice sounded in the helmets. "But I don't understand how you happen to speak English. It can't be your native tongue."

"Oh, no, Miss Mason. But we respond in whatever language in which we are addressed. It is only courtesy to do so."

Temple's liking for the weird creatures went up another notch. Apparently they could establish instant telepathic rapport that automatically adapted itself to any tongue. At the moment he had more pressing matters to explore.

"What is going to happen now? What will they do, and what are our chances?"

"Not good at all," the Vard said. "You should have carried away those other suits. They will send out humans to hunt us down with fearful weapons. Our masters dare not come out, but the minds of the hunters will be programmed to stalk us relentlessly. Meanwhile, you have no food or water. Your suits are poorly insulated against cold and your air supply is good for one hour only. This was purposely done so a slave could not break his bonds and remain outside."

Temple's eyes widened. "You mean it can be done? It is possible to wrest control from one of these entities?"

"Only humans have succeeded, and only those who resisted seizure so strongly that control was not complete. A mind taken unaware is powerless to escape."

Lee whistled. "Brother, if they try to grab me again, they are going to get the battle of their lives."

"I'm afraid we all are," Temple said. "Men in space suits are coming out of the air lock now. Can you help us, whatever your name is?"

101

"I am Decex Vard, which means my identification number is ten thousand. Wait here and I will try to locate a cave where the rocks give some protection."

He lumbered off at surprising speed. Temple could hear a soft clattering and realized it was Lee's teeth chattering. "I'm f-freezing, Curt."

"Enjoy it while you can," he said grimly. "When that sunshine reaches us, the temperature will go up to over two hundred degrees above zero. Then we'll really understand that old saying about out of the frying pan, into the fire."

The Vard came racing back. "I find no caves and the hunters are close. They bear our most powerful weapon, a beam that causes the atoms of anything it strikes to burst apart violently."

CHAPTER 16

Return To Captivity

"Come on," Temple said, gesturing. "Our only chance is to go up that crater wall. We can dodge the sun line longer and hide among the rocks."

They crossed the crater floor in great bounds, utilizing the lighter lunar gravity for added speed, dragging the aged Vard. An ache in his chest warned Temple that their limited air supply was nearly exhausted. High up the crater wall they flung themselves down, panting, behind a screen of rocks.

"We're nearing the end of the road," he said at last. "Then that lying Monj and his pack can go ahead with their non-conquest of Earth."

"Oh, no," Decex Vard said quickly. "You do not understand at all. My masters want only to return to their home. If it had not been for the failure of our poor bodies they would never have touched Earth. They discovered at once that the brief life span of humans could offer no clue to the salvation of our race."

Temple gaped at him. "Then why all this elaborate plot, the meteor camp, the Crimson Plague, the whole crazy, vicious hoax? If you know the answer, tell us."

"Of course. To construct the great ship for their return journey requires the labor of thousands of skilled hands and scientific minds. Yours are not the best, but they will have to do. The Crimson Plague, as you call it, is only our means of securing and protecting those who are needed on the moon to mine and process the special ores. Then we can move to the base on Earth and simply occupy as many bodies as necessary to fabricate the space craft and launch it."

The stunned silence was broken by Lee's strangled voice. "Then this whole horrible reign of terror was for no other purpose than to get the ship built so they could go home. Why in the name of heaven didn't the stupid idiots simply tell us their problem and ask for our help like gentlemen? The whole civilized world would have broken its neck to co-operate and speed them homeward."

Temple received a distinct impression that the Vard was close to a state of total shock. His voice was faint. "But—but, is yours such a strange race that you can *ask* for something and it is given *willingly*? That is contrary to natural law."

"The law of might makes right," Rocossen murmured dazedly.

"The law of seizure by conquest—the basic law of evolution. In their preoccupation with super-evolution, the Xacrns never discovered that there might be any other laws governing human nature. In science they are eons past us, but in human relations they're still back in our pre-dawn era of tooth-and-nail existence."

"What a colossal misunderstanding," Temple whispered. "What a grim cosmic joke. Now that I know, I can't even bring myself to hate them. I just feel sorry for the poor, dumb stupes. If I can talk to them, I'm sure we can iron this all out peacefully."

Lee had squirmed up to peer over the rocks. She came scrambling down, her face pale. "You'd better start ironing fast, then. The hunters are coming and, with no wind on the moon to disturb the dust, our tracks show up like Burma-Shave signs."

"Climb," Temple cried. "Stick to rocks where our tracks won't show. Here, Decex. I'll give you a boost."

The Vard shrank from his extended hand. Temple got an impression of embarrassment. "Please, I want to return to my master. Freedom was exciting, but I am lonely and afraid. Forgive me, kind humans, but those others are our people and they have given us much. They drive us to exhaustion and bring us pain, not because they are cruel but because they have evolved beyond feelings and emotions. Pain and fear, love and hate, are to them only words. We feel them only because we are not as far along on the scale of evolution. You have been kind and I appreciate it, but I must return to my own. Thank you and farewell." Before anyone could move he sprang up and went loping down the slope, like a many-legged lost dog.

Lee whispered, "The poor, simple, lovable dupe."

"That lovable dupe," Temple said harshly, "just showed some un-lovable dupes exactly where we're hiding. *Run!*" Before they could move there was a blinding, soundless flash and a gigantic rock a few yards away vanished into a puff of dust. Another above them succumbed to the titanic energy burst.

"Follow me," Temple shouted. "They'll have this shelter all blasted away in a minute. We'll be seen if we try to climb. Our only chance is to duck from rock to rock and try to get back to the dome. We've got to have fresh oxygen bottles. If I can keep you two alive out here while I go in and talk to them, there's a chance we can all survive. I think I know the answer to their problem."

"You can't stop the march of evolution," Rocossen panted.

"The hell you can't," Temple said harshly. "Our history is full of examples. Look at Greece, Rome, and Maya and Inca civilizations. They climbed far up the scale and then fell back."

Over their heads a giant pinnacle of rock exploded, then another

104

further back. Apparently they had not been seen and the hunters were only probing blindly. Temple climbed to a spot where he could look down onto the crater floor.

One of the hunters was almost directly below. He stood half turned, looking back along the wall, cradling his strange weapon as he searched. Temple beckoned the others. "There's one right below us and he's been allowed an extra oxygen bottle for this special chase. If we jump him together, we can get his air supply and smash that atomic gun."

The figure whirled, looking up. Temple realized, too late, that all the suits were probably on the same intercom band.

The weapon was lifting toward their hiding place. Temple kicked back against his rock and catapulted out in a headlong dive. He went plunging down with Lee's scream ringing in his ears.

The shock of his action slowed the hunter's movement for an instant. Before he could fire, Temple crashed into him. Even under the light gravity, the impact was stunning. His forehead smashed against the helmet with a force that brought tears to his eyes. The figure of the hunter sprawled limp and unconscious. He hurled the weapon far out and was unfastening the spare oxygen flask as Lee and Rocossen raced up.

"To the dome," he snapped. "This will keep you two going until I can dicker with Monj."

They went bounding across the crater floor, their suits winking with reflected star-shine. Suddenly the lava around them began to erupt in soundless bursts. With no betraying muzzle flash, there was no way to locate the unseen marksman. Before Temple could think of a counter-measure, another flash burst in their midst, sending them flying like tenpins.

They scrambled up, maintaining silence for fear of being heard, and started on. Rocossen suddenly staggered and collapsed. Temple ran to him, feeling a sharp knife of fear. "Rocky, how bad is it? Where were you hit?"

"Not—hit," the physicist panted. "Air—gone." One hand stirred feebly, pointing to a ragged gash in his metal breastplate. "Nothing to— patch with. You two—go on. I'll follow—if I can."

Temple shoved the extra oxygen flask into Lee's hand. "Run! Hide in that rock pile we ran to when we first came out. You can dodge around there until I get Rocky inside and talk to Monj. I'm safe from immediate seizure so I may have time to win him over and send help for you. It's our only chance."

Gathering the protesting astronomer in his arms he stumbled toward the air lock. Lee ran for the rocks, the soundless bursts following her flight. Temple stopped shaking when he saw her vanish into the concealing jumble.

With Rocossen's last air turned full on and both hands over the gash, he could eke out a few more minutes. Lunar gravity cut his weight to less than fifty pounds, but it began to feel like fifty tons to Temple, with his own lungs starving for oxygen. He staggered on, reeling on rubbery legs.

He was only vaguely aware of space-suited figures that were suddenly around him, relieving him of his burden, helping him on. He was barely conscious when he was dragged into the air lock, his helmet removed. Fresh, sweet air washed over his face. Sucking in deep breaths, he felt the mists lift from his brain but with maddening slowness. Vaguely he knew that his suit was being stripped off and that Rocossen was sitting up close by.

There was something wrong about the figure of the little physicist. Something was missing from an expected pattern. His fogged brain struggled with the mystery. The thoughts were all tangled with a desperate urging that was fighting to gain precedence. Something he had to say at once to Monj—something of vital importance. It was something about Lee Mason and about Plague victims and people who would gladly build a space ship.

The oxygen was beginning to clear his brain. Suddenly he remembered Lee waiting out in the rocks with a dwindling air supply and a stalking hunter.

He remembered the all-important thing he had to tell Monj—that he knew a solution to the Xacrn problem of defeating evolution. As soon as he explained, there would be no more Crimson Plague, no more mindless slaves, but only harmonious co-operation. Mankind would benefit by the awesome knowledge of the Xacrns and they, in turn, would have their space ship built for the journey home.

Last of all he realized what was different about Dr. Eno Rocossen. Grinning in triumph, the little physicist was standing over him, holding a curious instrument. He bent over Temple.

"This won't hurt, Curtis. It is a very superior form of anesthetic that will prevent your feeling a thing while the plate is being removed." His eyes again held the dead emptiness of an entity-controlled automaton. "Then you will be with us."

Temple tried to move, to shout. A puff of glowing gas whipped from the instrument and his senses drifted away. The last impression before blackness closed down was the voice of Monj, booming, "Take him to the operating room at once. I will operate without delay."

Panting and numb with cold, Lee crouched among the rocks, struggling with numbed fingers to replace her exhausted oxygen bottle with

106

the one taken from the hunter. The coldness of her body matched the coldness in her heart. Seeing Curt stumbling off across the alien landscape brought home the terrifying possibility that she had seen him for the last time.

She flinched instinctively as a rocky peak, only a few hundred yards away, vanished in a flash of unleashed fury. Moments later she saw the reflection of another flash, down low. The hunter was ranging the edge of the rock heap, trying to drive her from her hiding place. Another burst, almost overhead, showered her with debris.

On familiar Earth, Lee Mason was notably cool and nerveless in the face of danger. But here, in the lonely desolation of an alien, hostile world, she felt the impact of a nameless terror that could not be defeated by reason and logic. Another burst, even closer, brought sheer panic.

She scrambled up and ran, sobbing, blind with fear. A huge rock barrier loomed in her path. She gathered herself and jumped. Under gravity only one-sixth that of Earth, she went up to an impossible height and cleared it. Arching down, she braced herself against the impact of striking the ground in the black shadows.

There was no impact. She went down and down into a pit or shaft that seemed to have no bottom. Her tumbling body struck a rocky side and rebounded to another. Her ears were deafened by the grinding clatter of the metal suit against rocks. The tumult continued even after she struck bottom with an impact that jarred her senses.

She awoke gradually to a realization that she had fallen into a deep shaft that penetrated far below the crater floor. Only the lighter gravity had enabled her to survive at all in the thinly padded suit. As it was, her body was a mass of aches and bruises. She cautiously moved her arms and found them unbroken. She tried her legs and muffled a gasp of alarm. They moved but the legs of the suit did not.

Her exploring hands found the reason. She was almost buried under a mass of rocks dislodged by her fall. Only the strength of the metal suit had kept them from crushing her body. As it was, the rocks pinned her as solidly as a vise. No amount of straining could move one, nor could she free the legs of her suit.

She was hopelessly trapped—and somewhere in her panicky flight or fall, the fresh oxygen bottle had been irrevocably lost. Her chest was heaving as her lungs fought for the last tenuous molecules of oxygen left in the suit after her original bottle was exhausted.

A wild thought planted itself on her oxygen-starved brain.

"What a cold, lonely, horrible place to die."

CHAPTER 17

Journey's End

The group gathered in the smaller rocket tower of the meteor camp looked more like victims of a major catastrophe than distinguished scientists. Allen Farge was the worst, with two black eyes, a bent nose, missing teeth and his clothing in shreds. Mullane, Lansdon, Jacobs and the rest were almost as battered. The big Van Arden showed the least damage but he, too, had taken his lumps in the wild hand-to-hand battle in the doorway as the rocket blasted off with Temple, Lee and Rocossen.

They might still be fighting if Farge had not cleared enough elbow room to lift the projector and destroy the controlling entities. Now free, embarrassed and worried, they stared bleakly up at the split roof far above and considered the future.

"Damn," Farge cried hoarsely. "They're up there, either seized, dead or fighting unspeakable horrors and all we can do is stand down here like bumps on a log without lifting a finger to save them. Can't anybody in this aggregation of so-called eggheads come up with one, single, intelligent idea?"

"Easy, boy," Van Arden said. "We've used Lansdon's detector and your projector to root out and destroy all those things left here. The guards and the Solles are free and sleeping off their shock. Now all we can do is sweat it out right here. This is our only point of possible contact with—" He broke off, frowning, cocking his head.

There was a feeling of electric tension in the air and a thin, high, rising whine. In the gloomy shaft of the tower, a flickering turbulence was faintly visible. Mullane's wild yell broke the quiet.

"The rocket. It's coming through from the other dimension." He whirled to Farge. "Whoever's piloting will have to be under their control. Have your projector ready to blast when it opens."

Suddenly, soundlessly, the rocket was there, materializing out of thin air to awesome solidity. The lock began to open. In Farge's hand, the butt of the projector was clammy. Beside him, Van Arden muttered, "Don't miss. That crate is our only contact with the moon and we're going to ride it there if we have to paddle with our hats."

The lock chugged down, the gangplank lowering automatically to meet it. One of Farge's first projects had been to repair and restore that in preparation for a possible return of the ship.

Rocossen stepped from the lock and stopped, staring at the tense group with blank, suspicious eyes. Then his hand whipped from behind, leveling a blue beam projector. All saw the brief flash as Farge's weapon clicked first to destroy the entity.

The physicist tottered and dropped the projector and his unconscious figure pitched over the side of the gangplank to the concrete pit below. The thudding crash as his body struck was a death blow to their hopes.

When they reached him, he was unconscious and barely breathing. One arm and shoulder were broken, ribs smashed and there was more than a possibility of skull fracture.

In the control cabin, the scientists stared from the starkly plain control panel to one another with strained faces. Mullane was the first to speak. "I went back and forth once with Rocky but I can't remember what he did. I only know one thing. He said if there was the slightest error in passing through to that other-dimensional drive, the rocket and everyone in it would be instantly reduced to atoms."

* * * *

He had wondered often what it felt like to have his brain occupied and possessed by an entity. As Temple swung his feet off the operating table and stood up, he knew the answer at last, and tasted the full horror of that knowledge.

His sensations and feelings were normal. He possessed all his faculties except one. He had no control whatever over the thoughts that flashed across his mind or the commands they sent to his muscles. Across the chamber were two couches. On one the figure of Monj lay, apparently asleep. The other was empty.

Weary and shaken, he went to the empty couch to lie down and rest awhile. That is, his consciousness willed the movement but a stronger force made his tired body stand erect and turn the other way. There was nothing he could do to stop himself.

Dully he felt the back of his head. A small bandage was the only visible evidence of the operation. Apparently the skill of the surgeon body had been augmented by the superior Xacrn knowledge to make the operation simple, quick and without aftereffects. He wondered if he would even remember there had been an operation afterward—if there *was* an afterward.

Then full realization struck him. "I am a slave!" he thought wildly. "I belong to them."

An exultant reply flashed through his mind. "You belong to me— Monj. You are a more useful vehicle for my purpose than the other,

109

which I will keep for use when its skills are needed."

A frantic anguish tore at Temple. The lives and futures of the human race had been in his hands and he had let them slip, had unwillingly violated a trust. He had even figured out how to save the Xacrns from their doom—

In a flash of belated caution he blanked out the thought. That was his last and only bargaining hope, to be held back until he could be sure of fair exchange.

He had not been fast enough. Into his mind flashed a sharp, "What was that? What did you discover about our problem? Reveal your whole thought instantly or I will tear it from you, and I promise the process will not be painless."

Stubbornly Temple fought to submerge the thoughts. His mind and body reeled with the fury of Monj's rage. Probing tentacles tore into his mind like knives of fire, digging, gouging, wringing intolerable agony from hidden nerve ends.

Decex Vard had said that a strong and willful mind could sometimes resist an entity—but not one as all-powerful as Monj. Try as he would, fight as he could, the sinister force was reaching through, baring the last secret of his dwindling hope.

Suddenly the struggle ended, broken off by an incredible interruption.

The disheveled figure of Lee Mason burst through an archway. Her lovely face broke into radiant relief at the sight of Temple.

"Oh, Curt, thank God you're all right." She saw the figure that had been Monj on the couch. "You overpowered him somehow. I knew you could. Curt, you won't believe what happened to me. I fell down what must be a Vard mine shaft, lost my new air bottle and got my suit trapped by falling rock. Then I remembered air is heavy and collects in the lowest spots, so I unfastened my helmet and found I could breathe. I wriggled out of the suit and followed the shaft into a huge mine. There was a lighted corridor leading up so I followed it and here I am, with you."

Laughing happily, she ran toward him with outstretched hands. Behind Temple's false smile of welcome a titanic battle was raging. His whole being fought to cry a warning, while the mighty force of Monj kept him a silent Judas, waiting to grab her, tear off the silver cap and open her brain to entity.

His waiting hands closed like traps on her wrists...and something happened. A great surge of strength seemed to pour into his hands from the touch, her will rushing to join his. Against their united power, he felt the will of Monj waver and retreat. For moments they stood rigid, locked in savage battle.

Abruptly the battle ended as the entity gave up. Temple felt its bonds slip away and knew his mind was free again. He and Lee clung together for a moment of glad triumph.

The figure on the couch stirred and sat up, glaring in sullen hatred. Temple turned sharply. "Hold it, Monj. Don't try sending for a goon squad of human dupes, or you'll never learn the secret of saving your race. You know I found it and you know I'm not bluffing, because you glimpsed it in my mind."

"What do you want from me?"

"Your promise to keep hands off while I tell you the answer. And you'd better summon all your Xacrns to listen with you. Oh, yes, and I want that detector you swiped from me so I can see my audience."

A Vard shuffled in with the battered instrument and Temple knew he had an audience, even before the screen showed him the upper part of the cavern crowded solid with tensely waiting entities.

"Speak," Monj growled, "and it had better not be a trick."

"You know it isn't," Temple said, and his arms tightened on Lee's shoulders, drawing her closer. "You thought you knew all about our race, but you didn't know the basic principle of our whole civilization or you could have had the answer long ago. If you'd simply told your story, our whole world would have pitched in to help you, to build and stock your ship and see you safely off for home. We'd have done it without threats or pay because when the chips are down for somebody, that's the way human beings are."

Monj seemed utterly dazed, as the Vard had been, at such an incredible idea. Temple rushed on, "Your strong-eat-the-weak principle doesn't hold on Earth, except when some mad dog runs wild until decent people rise and slap him down. We feel one another's hurts and griefs and share his joys. We cry at sad pictures and lost kittens and send CARE packages to the underprivileged in lands we've never even seen. You can't understand that but you're going to have to in order to save yourselves. We call it the human spirit and it's the reason you could conquer the Earth but never conquer human beings. It's the tool that can rescue your race."

"Emotions," Monj growled. "Feelings. They are the mark of the lower orders, the primitives. We Xacrns left those behind with our equally useless bodies when we evolved into pure minds." His glare darkened. "But what is this great secret? You have not told us yet."

"I did, but you didn't see it," Temple said. "But now we do some dickering. Before I draw pictures for you so your feeble intellects can grasp it—" he grinned maliciously "—we talk about a few other matters. With our whole-hearted aid, how long would it take you to build

111

your ship and take off for Xacrn—with the secret you need for survival?"

"A week at most," Monj said, and his voice held a note of reluctant hope. "We would not need massive construction or fuel since we do not use your crude propulsion system. We only used a rocket on your world to lift us high enough so the turbulence of the space warp would not damage surrounding buildings. If we built the ship in an open field, we could flash almost instantaneously into the space-time dimension and emerge on our world. But the secret! If you know it, tell us."

"Not so fast, my lad. What can you, or will you, do to repair the damage you've done with your stupid bungling approach?"

"All humans will be returned to normal and those on the moon transported back to Earth at once. As for material damage, we give you the treasury of the moon and our rocket ships to use and to learn from. What you call Plague victims will be restored."

"Fair enough," Temple said. He sighed then smiled at Lee's happy face. "Then I give you the salvation of your race. Decex Vard, come up here to me."

The Vard lumbered hesitantly forward and Temple threw an arm across the leathery body. "When you reach home, do honor to this Vard, for he gave me the key to the secret. To survive, you must reverse your evolution and retrogress back from where you now stand on the brink of oblivion."

"Is that all you offer?" Monj cried. "We know that, but it cannot be done. We advanced to our present state by acquiring vast knowledge. But each new moment brings fresh knowledge, so we are swept onward against our will. We cannot erase what we have acquired, nor keep from learning more through each new experience."

"Maybe you can't erase," Temple said quietly, "but you can dilute that knowledge with other matter and get the same result. In the childhood of your race, thoughts and emotions were woven together in an inextricable bundle. You've gradually sorted out and discarded the emotional threads. Now you don't know what feelings are. You don't actually *fear* your own extinction, as we or a Vard knows fear. You only find it undesirable."

"And that's your answer. Use your Vards because you must and because they need you. But instead of ruling, try sharing. Feel what they feel, know what it's like to be weary and enjoy the pleasure of rest. You called emotions 'the mark of a lower order' but they are the stuff that will dilute pure mind and draw you back from the brink. As you merge with your Vards emotionally, you'll be retreating down the evolutionary scale a step or two—but without losing any gained knowledge."

He stopped, frowned, and suddenly could think of no more arguments, nothing more to add. "End of lecture," he said. "Period."

In the stillness he imagined the very atmosphere crackled with flying thoughts. Then Monj smiled and extended his hand. "It *is* the key. Will you shake hands, as your people do? I want to find out if I feel an emotion from it. If I do, our cure is already beginning."

Their hands met. "I believe I do feel it," Monj said. "Friends—forever friends."

His eyes bulged and his jaw fell. Temple whirled, hearing Lee's strangled shriek.

Bursting from the corridor to the rocket cavern came, without a doubt, the weirdest liberation army ever seen.

The bruised and battered Farge was in the lead, a silver loving cup split open and bound on his head with a scarf. At his heels Mullane wore a shapeless mass of hastily hammered silver from which protruded the tines of a silver fork. Jacobs wore a jingling cap of silver coins.

"We came to save you," Farge shouted. "Rocky's all smashed up out there, but he stayed conscious long enough to show us how to fly back here and wipe out this whole nest of devils."

He snatched out a projector, pressed the trigger and waved it grimly at Monj and every other figure in the cavern, then began systematically sweeping its invisible beam through the air above where he knew the entities hovered.

For a moment Temple was too stunned to move. Then a burst of crazy laughter came booming out of his lips. He howled, roared, slapped his thighs and finally choked, "Lay off, you wonderful dopes! That beam doesn't work in here on account of the shielding—thank the Lord. The war's over and everything is peaceful and friendly."

Monj pushed forward. "Your friend who is injured—let me go to him and use this surgeon's skill in a better cause."

Hours later, with Rocossen resting comfortably and the group at last convinced that the war was indeed over, they parted beside the rocket that waited to carry them back to Earth.

"I hope," Monj said, "that everything is settled now, with no matters left unfinished."

Temple looked startled. "Hey, there's some mighty important unfinished business, come to think about it." He pulled Lee into the curve of his arm and grinned at Monj. "There's going to be a wedding in the Culwain Chapel, and you're all invited, *friends*."

www.ingramcontent.com/pod-product-compliance
Lightning Source LLC
Chambersburg PA
CBHW032206190626
46810CB00018B/1872